The Black Tides of Heaven

JY YANG

THE BLACK TIDES
OF HEAVEN

A TOM DOHERTY ASSOCIATES BOOK

NEW YORK

THE BLACK TIDES OF HEAVEN

Copyright © 2017 by JY Yang

Cover illustration by Yuko Shimizu
Cover design by Christine Foltzer

Map by Serena Maylon

Edited by Carl Engle-Laird

A Tor.com Book
Published by Tom Doherty Associates
175 Fifth Avenue
New York, NY 10010

www.tor.com

Tor® is a registered trademark of
Macmillan Publishing Group, LLC.

ISBN 978-0-7653-9540-5 (ebook)
ISBN 978-0-7653-9541-2 (trade paperback)

First Edition: September 2017

To my queer family, who chill with me in the Slack

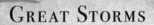
GREAT STORMS

ENDLESS SEAS

x.

GUSAI DESERT

BATANAAR

xv.

GAUR ANTAM

VISHARAN

vi.

TIGUMAN

ix.

NAM MIN

MATAPUR

ATHARAYABAD

viii.

EL ZAHARAD

THIEN CHIH

THE FIRE ISLANDS

DEMONS' OCEAN

THE QUARTERLANDS

KUANJIN

CHENGBEE

TESUGI
BAN

HATANAGI

iii.

ii

BUNSHIN

JIXIANG

i.

v.

RUYI

HAIFENG

vii.

YUGI

xiv.

MAHAPONG
CITY

ONGKOK

KATAU
KEBANG

MEKANTI

xiii.

xii.

CINTA
PUTRI

BANTURONG

BERENGI

MAP OF THE
PROTECTORATE

i. Tiegui
ii. Siew Tigui
iii. Mengsua Range
iv. Longfong Northern Range
v. Golden Phoenix
vi. Losang Range
vii. Jingpai
viii. Chac Mong
ix. Losang River System
x. Baoquan Lake
xi. Sisters Lake
xii. Sungei Bedarah
xiii. Sungei Sayagiri
xiv. White Plateau
xv. Kitesuaran Range

•||||||• = Mengsua Pass

Acknowledgments

Thanks to my editor, Carl Engle-Laird, and my agent, DongWon Song, for their faith in me and for making this novella duology work. To Irene Gallo, Christine Foltzer, and Yuko Shimizu, for the amazing cover, and for perfectly capturing Akeha's permanent level of grump. And to the crew sailing under the banner of Alyx, Kelly, Kelly, Jay, and Merc: you kept me afloat through the long nights of word processing. Thank you.

PART ONE

MOKOYA

Chapter One

YEAR ONE

HEAD ABBOT SUNG of the Grand Monastery did not know it yet, but this night would change the course of all his days.

He stood at the foot of the staircase leading to the Great High Palace of the Protectorate: that sprawling, magnificent edifice that few across the land would ever gain the privilege of seeing up close, much less entering. Tonight the Protector herself had summoned him.

Eight hundred alabaster steps stretched above his head. Tradition dictated that the journey to the palace be conducted without slackcraft, and Head Abbot Sung was nothing if not a traditionalist. There was no way around it, and so—he began to climb.

Darkness had fallen like a cool hand onto the peaks of Chengbee's exhausted, perspiring roofs. As the Head Abbot mounted step after step, his robes clung to him: under his arms, in the small of his back. The moon rolled uncloaked across the naked sky, but in less than an hour, the sun would return to scorch the land, bringing with it the start of the next waking day. On good days the nighttime exhalations of the capital city took on a lively air, the kind of energy that gathers where the young and restless cluster around the bones of something old. But all summer Chengbee had lain listless, panting like a thirsty dog.

Last summer, temperatures like these had wilted fields and dried rivers, turning them into brown gashes in the land, stinking of dust and rot. Fish bellies by the thousands had clogged the surfaces of lakes. The heat had brought on food and water rationing, the rationing had brought on riots of discontent, and the riots had brought the Protector's iron fist down upon the populace. Blood had run in the streets instead of rain, and the ruined fields were tilled with a fresh crop of gravestones.

The streets had stayed quiet this year. The Head Abbot found that this did not weigh on his conscience as much as he'd thought it would.

By the four hundredth step, the Head Abbot's breath was acid and his legs were lead. Four hundred more to go. No amount of meditation and training—not even a lifetime's worth—could compensate for old age.

Still, he climbed onward. Even a man of his stature could not defy a direct summons from the Protector.

And there was the matter of the debt she owed him from the last summer.

It was strange. The Protector had not been seen in public for several months now, and webs of rumors had been spun into that absence: She was ill. She was dead. Her eldest children were embroiled in a power struggle. There had been a coup by her ministers, some of whom had publicly voiced opposition to last summer's brutality. The Head Abbot had heard all these whispers, weighed their respective merits, and been unable to come to a conclusion.

At least now he could rule out the rumor of her death.

He ascended the last step with a great sigh. His legs were curdled jelly, and the entrance pavilion lay shrouded in a curtain of stars that danced and pulsed as blood slowly returned to his head.

Head Abbot Sung had grown up in a tiny village in the northern reaches of the Mengsua Range, a trading post of a mere thousand. The Great High Palace, with its wide court-yards and endless gardens, was easily three times the size of his home village. Its thousands of denizens—cooks and courtiers, administrators and treasurers—traveled from point to point on floating carts.

One such cart awaited the Head Abbot as his vision cleared. Standing beside its squarish, silk-draped bulk was someone he had hoped to see: Sanao Sonami, the youngest of Protector Sanao's six children. Sonami had just turned fifteen, yet still wore the genderfree tunic of a child, their hair cropped to a small square at the top of their head and gathered into a bun. They bowed, hands folded in deference. "Venerable One. I have been asked to bring you to my mother."

The Head Abbot bowed in return. "I hope you have been well, Sonami."

"As much as I can be."

The cart was just big enough for two seated face-to-face. On the inside it was shockingly plain, simple red cushions over rosewood so dark it was almost black. Sonami pulsed gently through the Slack, and the cart began to move, floating serenely over the ground. For one so young and untrained, their slackcraft had an elegance and a simplicity to it that the Head Abbot appreciated. As the white walls and wooden bridges of the Great High Palace drifted past the cart's embroidered windows, he asked, "Has your mother spoken to you about coming to the monastery?"

Sonami shook their head. "I only wish."

"I see." The Head Abbot had hoped that the summons were about the fate of the child—though perhaps "hope" was too strong a word when it came to matters concerning the Protector.

Sonami said quietly, hands folded together, "She has

decided that I should apprentice with the masters of forest-nature in the Tensorate."

"Is that so?"

The child stared at their feet. "She has not said it directly. But Mother has ways of making her wishes known."

"Well, perhaps our discussion today might change her mind."

"Discussion?" Sonami looked at the Head Abbot, alarmed. "Then no one has told you?"

"What have they not told me?"

"If you're asking, it means they haven't. . . ." The child subsided into their seat with a sigh. "Then it is not my place to tell you, either."

The Head Abbot had no idea what the child meant. *A mystery to be solved at the end of this journey,* he thought.

Sonami said, "When you agreed to help Mother with the riots last summer, what exactly did you ask for in return?"

"I asked for one of her children to be sent to the monastery."

"And did you say my name, specifically?"

The Head Abbot chuckled. "No one would be so bold, with such a direct request. I cannot imagine how the Protector would have responded. Of course, it was expected that she would send you eventually. That was what we had hoped for, wasn't it?" All her older children had already had their roles in the administration parceled out to them. Sonami was the only one left.

The child frowned and then looked out of the window. The cart was approaching a marvel of slackcraft: a massive square of water that stood unsupported, enveloping the center of the Grand Palace. A hundred yields high and a thousand yields in length and breadth, the moatcube was large enough to swallow fifty houses. Golden fish bigger than a child's head sluiced through crystalline turquoise.

Sonami tugged gently on the Slack, and the waters parted just enough to admit the cart. Curious fish swam around this intrusion into their habitat. The cart was headed for the innermost sanctuary of the Grand Palace, the place where only the Protector, her closest advisors, and her family were admitted. Head Abbot Sung had never seen it himself, until now.

The cart exited the water into the hollow center of the cube. A lifetime of purging emotion and base desire had not prepared the Head Abbot for the spectacle of the Protector's sanctuary. Stone floated on water, slabs of gray forming a base for a tessellation of square buildings woven out of wood of every color. Trees—cherry, willow, ash—entwined with one another, roots and branches knitting into nets through which light dappled: lantern light, dancing from the enormous paper globes that hung glowing in the air.

Then the Head Abbot realized that the trees and the buildings were one and the same. Some unknown Tensor architect had knitted living wood around stone foundations, folded them into right-angled, geometric shapes indistinguishable from traditional construction. Even the carvings on the ends of roof beams were live wood, guided into precise shape by slackcraft. Dragons and phoenixes and flaming lions lived and breathed and grew.

"It took a lot of work," said Sonami, to the Head Abbot's fresh, unbelieving intake of air.

"Did your mother do this?"

"No, I did." As the Head Abbot frowned, they added, "I, and a few others. But it was I who directed the design." The child looked out at their handiwork. "The old sanctuary was designed by someone who was purged after the riots. Mother wanted it changed."

"And she asked you to do it?"

Sonami nodded. "It was a test. I did not know it at that time, but it was."

"It's very well done."

"Mother says I have talents that are best not wasted. It's a rare gift, she says."

Sonami stopped the cart under the canopy of two intertwined cherry trees, one red and one white. As they disembarked, Sonami said, quietly, "You should not have given my mother space to interpret your request however she wished."

The child led the Head Abbot up a series of gentle stone steps. As he walked down a corridor of wood framed by windows of delicate silkscreen, the Head Abbot steeled himself. If the Protector imagined he would give up on their agreement without a fight, she was wrong. The ancient codes that governed such things ran deeper than the rivers and older than her blood. She could not throw them away so easily. To disrespect them would be to call into question the very nature of authority itself. And she, a descendant of foreign invaders into this land, would not want that.

She had promised the monastery one of her children, and she would give the monastery one of her children. The Head Abbot would see to that.

With a gesture, Sonami rolled aside the white silk door protecting their destination. Cool air gusted around the Head Abbot's ankles and neck, and enveloped him as he stepped inside.

And then he heard it: the high, thin wailing of a newborn.

A baby. A child.

The Head Abbot shut his eyes and silently recited a centering sutra before following Sonami past the privacy screens that had been set up in the room.

Protector Sanao reclined on a divan, supported by cushions of yellow silk, her face unpainted and her hair gathered cleanly in a bun on her head like a farmer girl's. She wore plain robes, the thick linen dyed dark blue, with none of the finery associated with her office. But she didn't need ornamentation to occupy the room as the sun occupies the sky.

"Venerable One," she said, her voice hard and smooth as marble, "I've brought you here to settle our debt from last summer."

The Head Abbot had already seen all he needed: the looseness of her robes, the flushed skin that spoke of her recent exertions. The mysteries that had plagued him like summer heat—her public disappearance, Sonami's cryptic remarks—unraveled like old yarn.

The Protector pointed, and one of her aides, a Tensor barely older than Sonami, ran forward to pull the red cloth off the woven basket on the table between them.

The Head Abbot knew what was in that basket, and he mentally prepared for the moment he had to look inside. Yet when that moment came, he blinked in surprise. Inside, swaddled in cloth, was not one red-faced, writhing infant, but two. One of them was crying; the other looked like it wanted to, but hadn't figured out how.

"Twins," the Protector simply said.

The Head Abbot looked at her and then back at the basket. Words would not come to him.

"You asked a blood price, and I am paying fully, and a little bit more. The fates conspired to double our blessings. Consider this gesture of generosity a measure of my gratitude for the monastery's support last year."

The crying infant stopped wailing to stare up at the Head Abbot. It had mismatched eyes, one brown, one yellowish. Its face crumpled in confusion, or some other unreadable emotion—it was only an infant, after all. Then it started crying again. Finally, the other twin joined in.

The Head Abbot's feelings swung like a pendulum. Anger at himself, for not having predicted this. Disgust at the Protector, for having done this.

The Protector folded her hands together. "They are yours now. Do with them as you wish."

"The Grand Monastery does not apprentice children younger than six," he said. And it was true. They had no facilities, no resources to deal with the unannounced arrival of two hungry newborns. "I will take them to one of the minor monasteries that has an orphanage, perhaps—"

"I did not birth these children to have them raised by nuns in some gutter district," the Protector said crisply.

Head Abbot Sung found himself at a loss for words again.

"Very well," she said. "If the Grand Monastery will not take them, I will raise them myself until they are six. You may return for them then." She gestured to the Tensor aide. "Xiaoyang."

The aide replaced the red cloth and took the basket away, disappearing behind the wall of painted silk that stood behind the Protector.

The Protector smiled at the Head Abbot like a tiger would. "I am sure you will find them adequate when you return," she said smoothly.

He stared at her.

"Do you contest the fulfillment of our agreement?"

"No, Your Eminence." He bowed in obeisance. What else could he do?

Sonami led him back out. They both settled into the cart and sat there awhile in silence.

The Head Abbot said to the somber child, "I am sorry."

Sonami shook their head. "You tried your best. Mother is Mother. She does what she wants."

"Indeed." He folded his hands together. "But I don't understand the purpose of twins." She must have had a reason for conceiving two children.

"It was an accident," Sonami said. "Conception through slackcraft has its risks."

"But why would she keep both infants?"

Sonami stared. "Mother is not *infinitely* cruel."

They started the cart moving again. As it slid back through the walls of water, Sonami said, "I will make sure the children are taken care of. I will look after them myself."

Their voice, although small, was cool and calm. The Head Abbot imagined that in maturity, Sonami might sound not so different from their mother.

He asked, "Will your mother allow that?"

"She will. I'll make sure of it."

The Head Abbot looked out at the marvels passing by without comment. How easily she had outmaneuvered him. He had stumbled in like a baby rabbit, eyes fused shut, and she had been the fox lying in wait, licking its chops. Here, at last, was the true face of the woman who had taken the derelict Protectorate of her ancestors—a feeble nation cowering in the shadow of almost-forgotten glories—and expanded it until her iron grip controlled more than half of known Ea.

Sonami said, "Venerable One, do you believe in the power of the fortunes?"

"Of course, child. They are what guides us and shapes the Slack."

The child nodded. "The fortunes didn't give Mother twins for no reason. That means that if there's a plan, she's not the one controlling it. And that does make me feel better." A small, brief smile overtook their face. "Perhaps this is for the best."

The Head Abbot blinked. This child, features still cushioned by the fat of innocence, spoke with the quiet confidence many took a lifetime to achieve. He had always suspected they were extraordinary, and not just because of their proficiency with slackcraft. When Sonami had first approached him with a desire to be admitted to the monastery, he had thought that with the right guidance, the child might one day grow up to take his place as Head Abbot, with all the secrets tied to that office.

Now none of them would ever know. That version of the future had been sealed off from them.

"Perhaps this is for the best," he agreed.

Chapter Two

YEAR SIX

THE MASSIVE CART THAT came from the Great High Palace was one of those that filled the width of streets in processions, painted lucky red and silk-draped in yet more red. Head Abbot Sung stood at the top of the stairs and watched its bright, meandering passage up the road that led to the Grand Monastery. The morning fog had long since retreated from the tree-embroidered mountains that formed Chengbee's backbone, and the light breeze scattered cherry blossom petals around his sandals.

The Head Abbot stood tall, but privately he was glad that the twins were coming to him, instead of the other way around. It was a long way down the mountain, and a long way up to the Great High Palace, and in recent years his knees had begun to hurt during the morning rituals and when thunderstorms were coming. The onset of age was like a dam breaking: slowly at first, then all at once.

Sonami was the first to exit the cart, a graceful figure wrapped in a light silk dress the color of chrysanthemums and jade. She had chosen her gender the same year the twins were born and had grown well into that role. As a young woman of twenty, she had her mother's height, and the fine features of her face bore more than a passing resemblance to the Protector's.

Two near-identical children tumbled out of the cart behind her, laden with packs. One landed with their soles a hip's width apart, fists lightly curled, balancing on the balls of their feet. The child with the mismatched eyes. The other one straightened up and stared at the Head Abbot with an intensity that was unnerving for one so young.

The Head Abbot bowed to them, and Sonami bowed back. "Venerable One," she said. "Allow me to introduce you to your new charges."

She touched the first child on their shoulder. "This is Mokoya." She tapped the second one, whose wide dark eyes remained fixed on the Head Abbot. "And this is Akeha."

"I welcome you to the Grand Monastery," the Head Abbot said. "Today you embark on a new journey of learning and discipline."

The children said nothing. The first child's face presented a scowl, while the second one didn't even blink.

"Go on," Sonami said gently.

A junior monk and nun waited behind the Head Abbot. "Go with them," he told the children. "They will show you to your rooms."

The children looked at each other, and the Head Abbot felt something pass between them in the Slack, as though they were communicating. He looked quizzically at Sonami, who only smiled.

The children seemed to come to an agreement, and that agreement was not to put up a fight. Silently and perfunctorily, they trudged after the waiting acolytes.

The first child, the odd-eyed one, took fewer than ten steps before their resolve shattered. They dropped their pack and ran back to Sonami, clutching the fine silk of her dress in their fists.

"Mokoya," Sonami sighed. She dropped to one knee and took the child's hands in her own. "We've talked about this."

"Why can't you come with us?" A tremor belied the stubborn pout in their voice.

"Because I'm going to the Tensorate academy. Today you begin training for monastic life. Head Abbot Sung will take care of you. All right?"

Their face folded up, equal parts rage and grief. Sonami said, "And you have Akeha. You have each other; you won't be alone."

The other child walked over and put a hand on their sibling's shoulder. The first flung themselves at Sonami in a desperate hug.

Sonami held them. "Go on. You know this is what Mother wants."

The child detached from Sonami's grasp and took their sibling's hand. Without a word, they marched, sibling and all, back to where the acolytes waited with the abandoned pack. The Head Abbot had expected tears, but none remained. They did not turn back to look at Sonami again.

The other child pinned the Head Abbot with an intense, baleful gaze as they walked by.

Sonami got to her feet with a sigh and watched the twins go. "They are good children," she said softly. "Understandably upset about leaving the only home they've ever known. But once the pain wears off, they'll give you no trouble." With a touch of amusement, she added, "Well, not much trouble, in any case."

The Head Abbot studied the young woman now standing before him. The two of them had barely spoken in the last five years; the Head Abbot's messages through the talker network had been gently but firmly rebuffed. He had tried for a long time to divine if this distance was the Protector's doing or Sonami's choice, but in the end had concluded that he had to respect and accept it. As with all things in life.

"You raised these children yourself," he observed.

Sonami nodded.

"I must confess I'm surprised. Did your mother not intend for you to enter the Tensorate before this?"

Sonami smiled slightly. "We agreed that I would do so after the children had been transferred to the Grand Monastery."

"Such concessions come with a price. What did you promise her in return?"

Her smile did not change as she said, "Grandchildren."

The Head Abbot swallowed his first response. Into his silence, Sonami interjected, "Of all her daughters, Mother was most interested in my gifts in slackcraft. She thought any children I had would have potential."

Carefully, he asked, "And this—you are happy with this?"

"It is how it has to be."

The Head Abbot sighed. Sonami laughed lightly. "Venerable One, I am glad the children will be given to your care. I am confident they will be well taken care of."

"Is there anything you want to tell me about them?"

Sonami hesitated. He watched intently as her answer percolated through layers and layers of careful thought.

Finally she said, "Do you remember you told me once that there was something different about me, as though the fortunes had embroidered a bright pattern in my soul?"

"I do." And he had believed it sincerely.

"At that time I dismissed it as flattery, something an old man would say to fool a young child. But . . . I think I understand now." Sonami frowned. "There's something about these children that's different. I don't know what it is. One of them . . ." The Head Abbot frowned, and Sonami shrugged. "I don't want to say too much. You will see for yourself. But I am glad that you will be directing their destinies, instead of Mother."

"I see."

"Trust in the fortunes," Sonami said. "They will guide you well."

Chapter Three

YEAR NINE

MOKOYA FINALLY MET DREAMS deep into the second night-cycle. Their breathing slowed and evened. Akeha opened their eyes surreptitiously, adjusting to the dark of the room, to confirm that their twin was indeed asleep.

Winter had silenced the frogs that sang outside the windows on warmer days. In that quiet, Akeha cautiously cleared their mindeye and tapped into the Slack. The world of arch-energies lay calm around the sleeping bundle of their twin. Mokoya had nightmares sometimes, and on those nights the Slack seethed around them like a wild river. But not tonight. In Akeha's mindeye, the Slack enfolded their twin like a gentle blanket, shimmering in the colors of the five natures.

If there were no nightmares tonight, then Akeha felt better about what they were about to do.

They left Mokoya sleeping in their shared bedroom and quietly slipped through the open doorway.

The sleeping quarters for initiates and junior acolytes were patrolled at night by Master Yeo, the disciplinarian, whose booming voice and bamboo switch they feared almost as much as her withering stare. Akeha caught glimpses of her silhouette patrolling the pavilion they had to cross, and shivered.

Akeha knew how to muffle their footsteps, thickening the air around their feet so that sound was silenced. But they had not yet figured out how to turn themselves invisible. The Slack was elastic, but not infinitely so. They had to think of something else.

A prayer altar sat a dozen yields away, garnished with the usual accoutrements. One of those was a tray of prayer balls, stacked into a silver pyramid.

There. First, they got into a runner's position. Then, with a tug through water-nature so small no one else noticed it, they toppled the prayer balls over.

Master Yeo whipped around and went to investigate the noise. Akeha streaked across the pavilion, unseen, while her back was turned.

Success.

Akeha tiptoed through the Grand Monastery, all the way to the vegetable gardens in the back, the soil bare and hard in the winter frost. Here, too, were the raptor enclosures, and as Akeha crept through the empty cabbage rows, the animals yipped excitedly, teeth and claws shining in the gloom.

"Quiet." A small gesture through the Slack calmed them. "It's just me."

The Grand Monastery was set against the hard spikes of Golden Phoenix Mountain, whose tree-covered sides formed a forbidding, fog-shrouded wall. Its grounds were protected by a slackcraft fence, humming electricity ready to shock anyone who tried to get past it.

Except here, next to the gardens. One of the charge devices generating the fence, a hollow ball filled with blue light, flickered in and out of service. The fence was broken.

No one had noticed. The device was supposed to sound an alarm when it failed or was tampered with. Somehow, that had not happened.

Akeha hadn't told anybody about this discovery. Not even Mokoya.

Now they hesitated. Mokoya would be upset that they were doing this. Several days ago their twin had woken, weeping, from a nightmare in which Akeha was attacked by a kirin in the mountain forest. Akeha had reassured them that firstly, kirin were extinct: nobody had seen one for a hundred years. And secondly, there was no way of getting into the forest.

Except now there was.

Akeha knew that if they'd told Mokoya about the

broken fence, Mokoya would have stopped them from going. So they had said nothing.

They stepped past the buzzing charge device and into the wilderness.

The forest whispered around Akeha. The sky was clear enough and the moon bright enough that they weren't afraid of getting lost. The ground changed as they wandered farther from the monastery, soft dry leaves yielding to mountain rock. Winter air bit at their exposed cheeks and knuckles.

Legends haunted Golden Phoenix Mountain. Akeha and Mokoya had spent hours in the Grand Monastery's library, thumbing through yellowed pages and absorbing them all. A diamond-studded road, it was said, led to a series of endless caves with alabaster walls, filled with sweet spring water and miraculous fruit trees that no person of the seas or the black-soiled lands had ever seen before. Akeha was determined to find out if it was true.

A path emerged from the unchecked wilderness of the forest. In the moonlight the pebbles embedded in its dirt shone like diamonds.

Akeha followed it. The path led them on a gentle climb that threaded along the mountain's slope. The trees parted, but the forest remained thick around them.

Every now and then, they would look up through the netting of leaves, tracking the moon's passage across the sky. They had to stay aware of the time. They couldn't get caught.

Akeha came to a small clearing in the forest, a break in the tree cover. The path they had been following forked here, one branch headed downhill, and the other headed up, into the depths of mountain territory. If there were secret caves in the mountains, Akeha thought, the second path would surely lead them there.

Something moved behind them, a large and unexpected presence. Akeha froze, and listened.

The forest breathed. Still. Silent. Akeha counted numbers as they waited, but there was nothing. It was just their imagination.

There was that sutra, the First Sutra, that Mokoya liked to recite in their head when they were nervous: *The Slack is all, and all is the Slack,* and a long-winded list of nonsense about the five natures. Akeha had a better, shorter list:

> *Earth, for gravity;*
> *Water, for motion;*
> *Fire, for hot and cold;*
> *Forest, for flesh and blood;*
> *Metal, for electricity.*
> *Everything else is extra.*

They breathed in, and out. Cleared their mindeye, and—

The kirin lurched out of the shadows at the same second they felt its presence in the Slack.

Akeha jumped backward, tripped foot over foot, landed on the flat of their palm. Pain shot up their arm. The kirin reared, wings swallowing the sky, head brushing the top of the trees, screech shaking the bones of the earth. A creature that was half bird, half lion, and all terror.

Akeha panicked. They'd never fought anything this big before. The creature before them was a blinding light in the Slack, sinew and flesh and bone. And blood. Warm blood surged through its veins. Overwhelmed by terror, they could only think, *I have to stop it.*

They tensed through water-nature, slowed the flow of blood by force, and stopped the kirin's heart.

The kirin shrieked in pain. Startled, Akeha let go. They'd never heard anything scream like that before. Their stomach twisted, heavy and sour.

And then the kirin staggered as if struck, as power surged through the Slack from somewhere else. The creature fell to its knees, missing Akeha by a handsbreadth. Its breath was hot on their face.

With a noise that was both a groan and a cry, the kirin staggered to its feet and retreated into the trees. Badly hurt or just badly shaken, the creature had had enough. Akeha watched it vanish into the shadows, the rustle of its passage fading.

Mokoya stood on the path behind them, trembling, wide-eyed, and angry. Akeha got slowly to their feet. Their arm sang with pain where it had broken their fall. "How did you find me?"

"I told you. I saw you in the dream."

"It was just a dream."

"It *wasn't* just a dream. I saw it exactly like it happened. When I woke up, you were gone, and I knew where you went."

And Mokoya had predicted the kirin, too. The creature was supposed to be extinct. But they had known it would appear. How?

Akeha frowned. "Are you saying you dream about the future? Only prophets do that." There hadn't been a prophet recorded in the Protectorate for hundreds of years.

Mokoya bit their lip, and Akeha recognized that expression. Their sibling was one surge of anger away from tears. They grabbed their twin's hand, balled into a hard fist that would not relax. "Moko."

"You could have died. What were you doing?"

Akeha glanced toward the hidden peak of Golden Phoenix Mountain. "I was looking for the hidden caves."

"Why?"

They shrugged. "We need somewhere to run if Mother comes to take us. I don't want to go back."

Mokoya pulled their hand away. "She won't come. She doesn't care about us."

They turned so that Akeha couldn't see their face. But Akeha knew with absolute clarity that they were more frightened than angry. The twins had a sense of each other, of emotions and anxieties, and they could hear each other's voices through the Slack if they listened hard enough.

"Don't be frightened," Akeha said. "I'll protect you."

"Protect me from what? The future?"

"Anything."

Mokoya turned back, cheeks painted with damp streaks. "What if it's true? What if I'm dreaming about things that haven't happened yet?"

"I said anything," Akeha repeated, and pulled their twin into a fierce hug that blanketed up all protests. "We don't have to tell anyone. It can be our secret."

Mokoya settled into the hug, but their mood remained rough and shaky, and Akeha knew they weren't convinced or comforted by that, either. "Let's go back," Akeha said. "Before anyone notices we're gone." The ache in their arm had almost subsided, and the fear and nervousness had faded into whispers. They could pretend that nothing had happened.

~

It was the sobbing that woke Akeha. All night they had floated on the edge between sleep and consciousness, plagued by visions of nightmarish shapes. Now their twin was hunched over at the edge of their shared sleeping mat, skinny frame shaking in the dark.

Akeha crawled over and tapped them on the shoulder. When Mokoya didn't respond, they shifted so that the both of them were face-to-face. Mokoya's was a crumpled, runny mess of fear and desperation. Another bad dream: the Slack seethed with the stress that trailed in the wake of their twin's nightmares. It had been weeks since the last one, but the intensity of the dreams seemed to be getting worse.

Mokoya stopped to gulp down two lungfuls of freezing night air, then continued crying. Akeha reached out and took their hands and said nothing. This was becoming a familiar routine.

Eventually Mokoya's sobbing petered into small sniffles. They wiped their snot with a thick sleeve as Akeha asked, "What's happening?"

They shook their head, lips still sealed. Akeha pressed on: "What did you see?"

"Bad things."

"I know it was bad things. What kind?"

Mokoya could not meet their eyes. "I saw a naga."

"Where? Here?"

Mokoya shook their head. "At the spring procession."

The spring procession was in two weeks, in the center of Chengbee. As Akeha considered this bit of information, Mokoya said, "You were there."

"Why would I be at the spring procession?"

"I don't know, you were in the forest too, how am I supposed to know what's going to happen, I don't control any—"

"Okay, okay. There's a naga at the spring procession. I'm also there."

"We were both there."

"Of course. What happened?"

"It fell. The naga. It was flying, it took over the sky. Something happened. It fell onto the houses."

As Akeha frowned, Mokoya added, "People got hurt."

"Why did it fall? Was it attacking the city?"

"I don't know," Mokoya hissed, and their expression, which had been approaching normality, slid back toward furious tears. "I just saw it."

"Did you get hurt?"

Mokoya buried their face in their hands, fingernails digging into the skin. "I don't know. It just happened."

Akeha gently pulled their hands away from their face. Mokoya put up a token resistance, and their hands slowly uncurled in Akeha's. "Listen," they said. "That was just a silly dream. Naga don't come this far north. They live in the unknown south, in the Quarterlands, right? Even when they get lost, they don't go farther than Katau Kebang. They can't reach Chengbee. It's impossible."

"Nothing's impossible."

"Well, somebody will see it, right? And then they'll catch it. So it won't happen."

"It was really big, Keha. Naga are really big."

"I know."

"You said the same thing about the kirin."

"That was different."

"You said kirin don't exist anymore. And there was one. Just as I saw in my dream."

Akeha sighed and let go of Mokoya's hands. They were right. There was no easy explanation that could wave away what Mokoya had seen.

The twins looked at each other in the half-dark chill, not daring to voice their fears. There was always an explanation, that was what they had been taught, that was the way they had been raised, but this—the Slack was doing something strange to Mokoya, when it shouldn't.

"We need to tell somebody," Mokoya said.

This time it was Akeha's turn to ball their hands into fists. "And who are we supposed to tell?"

"One of the adults." As Akeha's face worked into a

scowl, Mokoya said, "We have to tell someone. We can't fix this by ourselves."

"Who says we have to fix anything?"

"People are going to get hurt if we do nothing, Keha. I have to tell someone."

Akeha hated the way Mokoya emphasized the word "I." It was a clear division, almost a threat. Hadn't they agreed to do everything together? "They're not going to believe you."

"They will. The Head Abbot will."

"And if he believes you? What happens then? Do they call you a prophet?"

Mokoya coiled their shoulders in a shrug. "I don't know. Who cares? It's more important to stop the dream from happening."

Akeha sat back on their heels and blew a hot breath through their teeth. They weren't sure what to say.

"I'm going to tell him tomorrow," Mokoya said.

"Fine." Akeha unfolded from their crouch and went back to their side of the sleeping mat. They could sense Mokoya's stare as they curled up on the roughly woven surface and shut their eyes.

"Are you angry with me?"

"No," they said, but they didn't turn around. "Go back to sleep."

Chapter Four

AKEHA PROWLED THE INN'S upper-floor balcony. The creaky strip of wine-stained wood overlooked the thoroughfare through which the spring procession clanged, swayed, spun, and marched. On either side, the balconies bulged with cheering, laughing, red-cheeked citizens. In contrast, this one was still and silent, lined with a full troupe of pugilists hand-selected from the most senior acolytes in the Grand Monastery. And then there was the Head Abbot himself, breathing slowly and evenly, calm and implacable as a mountain.

"Stop that," Mokoya hissed, as Akeha turned on an impatient foot to begin a new circuit of the balcony.

Mokoya had lied to the Head Abbot in order to bring them all here. They'd said nothing about the kirin in the forest, or the broken fence. Instead they claimed to have foreseen the incident last week where two of the junior acolytes broke the statues of Patience and Gratitude that guarded the front pavilion. Akeha had laughed about them lying to an adult, and had gotten kicked in the shins for their trouble.

More surprising was the fact that the Head Abbot had believed them without question. Every now and then, Akeha caught him staring across the length of the balcony at Mokoya, whose gaze was trained unwaveringly on the sky. Akeha felt like he knew something, something he wasn't telling either of them.

They rocked back and forth on the balls of their feet, humming tunelessly. Mokoya glared.

Downstairs, the procession continued on its multi-hued, clamorous way, unaware of the tensions strung overhead. The dancers and floats would thread their way through Chengbee's ant-nest streets before passing by the Imperial Square, to present themselves to the Protector and the upper echelons of the Tensorate. The Protector's family were expected to be in attendance as well. Sonami would be there. Everybody would.

Everybody except for us, Akeha thought. Did they even count as the Protector's family anymore?

Nearby, Mokoya went suddenly still and alert. *What is it?* Akeha thought at them.

I don't know. It's something.

The empty skies darkened from gray to blue as sunfall came. Along the thoroughfare, sunballs winked to life, illuminating the excitement-flushed crowd with a soft glow.

Wasn't it at sunfall, your vision?

Mokoya squinted at the sky, as if they were trying to listen to a small scratching sound from very far away.

Akeha moved so that they stood side-by-side, the edges of their palms brushing. It was easier to clear their mindeye like this, with their twin as a steadying, calming anchor.

They remembered the way the kirin had appeared to them, a blaze of light so bright it seemed to squeeze the Slack around it. People shone on the surface of the Slack, but not like that. Not that intensely.

If the naga was the same way, they would feel it in the shape of the Slack before it appeared. Sinew and flesh and bone and blood. Akeha concentrated, trying to widen the scope of their mindeye as much as possible, see as far as possible in the Slack—

There. There, Moko, there!

The distortion in the Slack was moving fast, like a meteor, destructive, and the light was coming toward them like a transport headlight down a tunnel—

Sinew. And flesh. And bone. And blood.

The naga was massive, wingspan of ten houses, clawed feet and barbed tail, mouth big enough to swallow a person whole. It was more raptor than serpent, hollow-boned and warm-blooded. That blood rushed swift and strong as a monsoon river. It called to Akeha.

They focused on that blood as the naga burst over the horizon, over the tops of roofs, blocking out the screams because they had to get the timing exactly right—

Akeha clenched their fist, and the raging torrents of blood froze.

The naga's scream thrust like a spear through the eardrums. The massive creature twisted in the air, and Akeha opened their eyes to see it coming toward the inn like a hailstorm. Their breath caught.

Someone grabbed them by the collar. "Jump!" was the instruction. The Head Abbot had pulled the twins together, and Akeha jumped, their legs and body going numb as things collapsed around them. Not just the inn, which rained planks and splinters and bricks around them as they hit the ground with a bone-shattering thud. Everything fell.

Akeha struggled upright, getting off the ground, trying to see the damage that had been done. Pain shot through their ankle, and they stumbled. Something reached around them: Mokoya, holding them up with trembling arms.

The naga had come down on the row of houses where the inn used to be. It groaned, a wild rumbling sound, but the light it burned in the Slack was fading. Sunfall was complete. The shapes of people ran to and fro in the darkness, some screaming, some holding their heads. One of the procession dancers wailed and screamed as she tried to push a block of wood, a broken pillar, off the shape of another dancer crumpled on the ground. Surprisingly, there was no blood. The lights festooning the dead dancer's dress still glowed and sparkled, as if nothing had happened. They had lost a shoe as they fell.

Oily smoke crept through the air as the sounds of crackling—like offerings for the dead—rose up around them. Or was it merely the rushing of blood in Akeha's ears? Mokoya was shaking them, saying syllables that wouldn't gel into words.

Things had happened exactly as Mokoya saw them. Why hadn't they realized this?

~

One night-cycle after Mokoya's whimpering had been silenced by unconsciousness, Akeha admitted to themselves that they were not following their twin into sleep at all. They slowly sat up in the gloom, careful not to disturb the shallowly breathing mound next to them.

The half hour before the sun returned to the skies was the coldest. Two night-cycles had passed, and a whole new day approached. Akeha's fingers were numb, and their vision shone with waves of exhaustion, but rest and darkness would not come. Their mind would not settle.

Akeha, separated from their twin, had spent nearly two hours being questioned by the senior acolytes and the Head Abbot himself, passed around like cracked tableware. They repeated their story over and over: They had not intended to kill the naga. They wanted to send it away. Once or twice, they had almost slipped and mentioned the kirin in the forest, where they were not supposed to have been. But they caught themselves in time.

Eventually they had been allowed to return to their bedroom, where they found Mokoya sitting with their chin tucked against their knees, expression blank. And then they had to explain, for the final time, that they hadn't really meant to kill the naga. They hadn't meant to make the prophecy come true.

Akeha watched Mokoya as they slept. For once, they were not sure what their twin believed. No, Mokoya was not obliged to talk to them. And they were probably as tired as Akeha was, and frightened too.

But they wished Mokoya had said *something*.

Akeha got to their feet and shuffled toward the door. There was no point in lying still and trying to fall asleep. They knew it wouldn't happen.

They crept around the austere gray sprawl of the Grand Monastery, letting the cold slow their blood and heartbeat where their mind wouldn't. These were the wide corridors they and Mokoya had breathlessly run down between lessons, the stones upon which they had both sat for hours meditating, the courtyards in which they had sparred, using sticks and slackcraft as weapons.

Akeha's childhood memories of the Great High Palace stitched together snatches of color and heavy fragrances with zither song and faraway, gentle laughter. They used to feel a jolt of strong, unnamable emotion whenever they thought about it, but those emotions had faded as the seasons left, and came back, and left again. The Grand Monastery was their home now.

A circle of light glowed in the distance, glimpsed between the even wooden teeth of intersecting corridors. The Head Abbot was not yet asleep.

For reasons they couldn't quite understand, Akeha found themselves creeping toward the Head Abbot's quarters. As they got closer, they heard voices: the Head Abbot had a visitor. In the deepest part of night.

Akeha shuffled into a crouch and pressed against the wall of the Head Abbot's room, underneath the window. Their heart pulsed in their throat: if they were caught, they didn't know what they would say.

"This is a generous offer," said a high, crisp voice. Akeha's memories of the Great High Palace came unbound in a wild cascade. That voice belonged to bright, wide halls with climate control and murmuring, attentive audiences. Second Sister Kinami—wasn't she the Chief Royal Diplomat now, overseeing the Ministry of Diplomacy whose fingers stretched everywhere the Protectorate held land?

"It's hardly an offer," the Head Abbot said. "I'd call it a demand."

"Well, you know Mother. Negotiating is not one of her great interests."

"We made a compact, a blood deal. She cannot simply back out of it as it suits her wishes."

"Except she isn't backing out of anything. She promised you one child. She gave you two. At the end of it, you'll still have one."

Akeha dug their nails into their palm to stop from shaking. One leg was already feeling the strain from the unnatural crouch.

Kinami said, "Mother has requested only the prophet's return. You can keep the other one. That fulfills the terms of the deal."

"You speak of them as though they are mere numbers on a ledger. They're *children*. You cannot just move them from one column to the next."

Silence from the other end. Akeha could imagine the cold, arch expression on Kinami's face. Of all their older sisters, Kinami was the closest in temperament to Mother, and even as a small child, Akeha had hated her. The Head Abbot had to tell her no. Tell her to go away.

"I see. I suppose I should have expected this. After all, treating people like numbers *is* one of your mother's specialties."

Akeha scrunched their face up to keep from screaming. Of course the Head Abbot wouldn't fight Mother's wishes. Nobody would.

"You'll have a week to make the arrangements. Let the prophet say their good-byes. It should be plenty of time."

The meeting was ending. Akeha had to get away. They kept to their crouch for two steps, and then started running, head ducked, chest constricting in pain. Wooden floorboards creaked as their soft-soled shoes slapped over them.

By some miracle, Akeha got back to their room without being stopped. They crashed against the wall next to the door and slid to the floor, gasping, their calves burning.

Mokoya sat up, robes mussed and eyes wide. "What happened? Keha? What is it?"

The conversation between Kinami and the Head Abbot repeated in Akeha's head in a deathly loop. "They're coming for you."

"Who?"

"Mother. The Tensorate."

Mokoya struggled to clumsy feet, wiping the sleep from their face. "For us?"

"No. Just you."

Mokoya froze as though struck by lightning. "They can't do that."

Akeha pressed their head into the wall's unyielding surface and closed their eyes. They felt tired, all the way deep in their neck and shoulders and head. Their muscles shook, their heart wouldn't stop beating. "They can do whatever they want."

"No." Mokoya's voice was soft but determined. Akeha felt fingers close around their hand and tighten vise-like. "Keha, we have to do something."

Chapter Five

THE MOON RULED THE skies as the children set out past the guardians of their sleeping quarters, past the empty vegetable garden, past the raptors and through the broken fence. When it was just them and the forest again, Akeha stopped to adjust the heavy pack they had strapped on. Their exertions clouded the air with white puffs.

"Come on," Mokoya hissed. "We need to get as far as possible before they realize we're gone."

Akeha hesitated, and they said, "*Keha.*" Then they turned and set off into the wooded depths without checking to see if Akeha followed.

Mokoya's steady gait never wavered, retracing the route they knew: through the trees, toward the shining path that led up to the peak of the mountain.

"If the kirin comes back, you'll kill it, won't you?" Mokoya said, as they walked.

Akeha didn't reply. They were mentally counting the biscuits and dried rice cakes stuffed into the packs, five days' worth of stealing from the monastery's kitchens. It would last them three days, four if they skipped meals. And they needed to find a source of clean water sooner than that.

Akeha had lagged behind, footsteps slowed by thought. Mokoya stomped over, and it was almost a shock when they seized Akeha's hand. "Keha. We have to stay together."

"This is a mistake," Akeha whispered. "Let's go back to the monastery."

In the moonlight, Mokoya's face looked sharp and angry. "And let them take you away from me?" Even though the exact opposite was happening. "I'd rather die."

Akeha pulled their hand away. "Stop spouting rubbish."

"I'm not going back. Mother can't do whatever she likes. I'm not a token on her chessboard."

"I told you," Akeha said bitterly. "You shouldn't have said anything about your dream."

"And *you* shouldn't have killed that naga."

Akeha peeled their lips back and hissed. That was enough. They turned their back to Mokoya and headed the way they'd come, feet slipping on the brittle dead leaves that had lain there all winter.

"*Keha.*" Mokoya lunged after them and grabbed their arm with both hands, fingers pressing through the layers of cloth hard enough to bruise. "I'm sorry, please, don't leave me."

Akeha wriggled out of Mokoya's grasp, but stayed where they were. "Don't be stupid." They could no more leave their twin alone here than they could cut off their own arm.

They stood like this for a moment, two children lost against a backdrop of endless forest. The weak foliage shadow shifted uncomfortably as the moon rolled across the sky.

"You lead the way," Akeha said.

Mokoya pointed. "The path's over there."

The sun rose, fell, and rose again as the children walked. A dull pain spread through Akeha's soles, but they focused on putting their feet down, one after another, on the stone-studded path that led them up the mountainside. As the path dipped into a crevasse of rising granite walls, their calves and back started to cramp.

One sun-cycle later, they stopped to eat and rest. Akeha rotated their ankles, dismayed by how everything hurt. They had been walking for little more than half a day.

"There should be some caves up there," Mokoya said, pointing into the half dark, where the path disappeared upward around a steep mountain face.

"Did you see that in a dream?"

"No," they said, annoyance creeping into their voice. "I just have a feeling."

Akeha leaned their head against Mokoya's shoulder and shut their eyes. Their twin was right, it did feel damper around here, like there was resting water close by, and that could mean caves. Or something. They were tired of arguing.

Mokoya put an arm around them.

"They should be looking for us by now," Akeha said.

"We should go," Mokoya murmured.

So they packed up and continued on the path. It was alarming how fast the aches returned to their bodies. Mokoya was limping, heavily favoring their left leg.

"Are you hurt?" Akeha asked.

"It's just blisters." They stopped. "Keha—look!"

Mokoya pointed. White mist was lifting from the crags and hollows of the earth. In the distance, the path vanished into a slender mouth in the rock.

They'd found a cave. Against all the odds, they'd found it.

Mokoya picked a branch off the ground and tugged at fire-nature to light it. The mouth of the cave was steep and littered with sharp rocks which skinned Akeha's palms as they scrambled up.

"Keha. Look."

Mokoya held the improvised torch aloft in the cave mouth. The roof yawned fifty yields above their heads, thick with the chittering of bats. Somewhere in the vicinity, water ran, echoing off stone walls. Step by small step, the two children moved inward, sheltered in the torch's circle of safety.

"It's strange," Akeha said.

"What is?"

"The floor is clean." With all the bats singing above them, they should have been walking across a carpet of droppings. But their circle of light showed nothing.

Mokoya looked up. "There's a barrier," they said after a while. "Slackcraft."

"Someone else comes here."

"It has to be."

"You think they live here? In the wild?"

"I don't know." Mokoya frowned. It was too late to turn back. "We'll find out."

As they ventured farther in, the walls of the cave opened up into a space huge enough to kill echoes. A breeze lingered around Akeha's neck, its cold breath raising gooseflesh. Mokoya sucked in a breath. "Look."

The dim shape of wooden crates, stacked upon one another, populated the cave floor. Akeha sent a cautious tendril out through the Slack and discovered warm pinpoints that responded to their slackcraft. A string of sunballs. Akeha tensed through metal-nature, and their glow filled the room.

"Great Slack." Mokoya put the torch out as hundreds

of heavy wooden crates, reinforced by tempered iron, revealed themselves. "What are they?"

Several years' worth of dust coated the boxes. Akeha left long finger streaks across the top of one. It wasn't labeled. As gray clouds danced around them, Akeha lifted the hinged lid. It was heavy, but it wasn't locked.

The crate was stacked with lightcraft in the shape of lotuses, like the kind Akeha had seen some of the senior acolytes use in aerial sparring practice. Unlike the weathered equipment back in the monastery, these hadn't seen much use. They looked thicker and stronger, too. Akeha touched one with slackcraft. There was barely any charge left, and whatever threads of metal-nature had been used to weave the energy in place had long since frayed.

Mokoya had pried open another crate, a long boxy one the shape of a coffin. "What are these?" They reached in and pulled out a long, thick metal rod, like a cudgel. The black carvings across its surface caught the yellow light as Mokoya experimentally twirled it.

"It looks like a weapon," Akeha said. Mokoya had had the same thought, moving into a fighting crouch, cudgel balanced in two hands. It was too long for them: an adult's weapon.

The cudgel hummed as Mokoya charged it with slackcraft. Neither twin had seen anything like it before.

Mokoya swung it above their head with practiced ease, despite its length. "There must be hundreds of these," they said, as they tilted it back and forth, examining it. "Why?"

"They're war supplies," Akeha said.

Mokoya blinked. "War? What kind of war? There hasn't been a war for years."

"Does it matter what kind? There are no good kinds of war."

Mokoya looked troubled by this, and started swinging the cudgel again.

"Be careful," Akeha warned, as the cudgel missed one of the crates by a fingerswidth.

As Mokoya swung the cudgel through another rotation, one end clipped Akeha in the shoulder. "You oaf," Akeha spluttered, and kicked up the sand on the cave floor and sent it sweeping in a wave toward Mokoya.

The assault through water-nature sent their twin staggering. Mokoya fell, but was back on their feet instantly, growling. They jabbed the cudgel in Akeha's direction.

The cudgel caught the thread of Mokoya's slackcraft. It hummed, glowed, and a bolt of electricity arced from it and struck Akeha in the chest.

Akeha went crashing to the ground, stunned, as though someone had dropped a boulder on them. Their chest burned.

"Keha!" Mokoya dropped the cudgel and ran stumbling toward them, sliding on their knees across the cave floor. "Keha, say something. Keha, please."

They couldn't. Their chest hurt too much. Akeha tried moving their arms, tried sitting up, and doubled over in pain.

Something growled deep and low behind them. Mokoya's eyes widened; their fingers trembled on Akeha's arm.

A familiar shape moved into the circle of lights. As Akeha struggled onto their elbows, trying to work past the bolt's paralyzing effect, the kirin reared up and screeched.

The creature lunged. Everything moved in a blur: the talons coming down, Mokoya throwing themselves over Akeha. Akeha tensed—Was it by instinct? Or something else?—and energy surged through the Slack, water-nature, as they shoved Mokoya away, before the kirin's clawed feet struck—

The talons went through their side like it was paper. Akeha screamed, sensations burning through them. A clear and precise epiphany struck: They were going to die. There was no turning back. It was done.

Their blood soaked through layers of clothing as they lay on the ground, gasping, barely holding on to consciousness.

A crackle through the air, sharp smell of metal burning. The kirin screamed, and its limbs folded. Mokoya had picked the cudgel up. As the creature struggled to its feet, Mokoya struck it again. And again. And again. Their twin blazed with such fear and anger it punched through the wall of pain surrounding Akeha. They hit the kirin until it collapsed thrashing to the ground, until the convulsions subsided into twitching, until it fell heavy and still. The air reeked of burning flesh.

Akeha watched this all through a veil of increasing darkness. The world grew cold, and the pain was, at last, fading away. They were aware of Mokoya picking them up, screaming, pressing their head against their belly. Akeha was drifting away, and as they grew distant from their body, they began unraveling in the Slack, becoming pure energy.

Something pulled them back. Mokoya was tensing through forest-nature, trying to knit the torn flesh back together, trying to keep their failing heartbeat steady.

Akeha reached out through the Slack. Mokoya was so bright, so beautiful. Like a jewel shining, like a sunset over the sea. *It's okay, Moko. It's better like this.*

No. Keha, no. You have to. You can't die. I won't let you.

Now you can go back to the Great High Palace. You don't have to worry.

I can't, I won't. Mokoya was crying so hard their body

was shaking. They could not have spoken if they wanted to. *If you die, I want to go with you.*

I don't want that. You have a good life ahead of you. Moko—

What's the point? What's the point of it?

Akeha struggled not to drift away entirely. They couldn't leave Mokoya like this. *It's too late, Moko. You have to go on. I want you to.*

The cavern filled with the sound of buzzing—a light-craft in operation. Of all people, the Head Abbot appeared, sailing in like a bird, serenity turning to alarm as he took in the scene before him. How had he found them? A question for another time. The old man leapt off the lightcraft and hurried toward the twins.

A cool hand pressed against Akeha's forehead, and warmth ran through them, healing warmth, tying them more securely to this world. "They're still breathing," the Head Abbot said. "We can save them. What happened? The kirin?"

Mokoya's lungs operated in desperate gasps. "I killed it."

"I know, Mokoya. She was one of the very last of her kind. She was trying to protect the cache. Don't worry, you are both safe. Help is coming."

Their twin formed words between the heaves of their chest. "I don't want to be taken away. I don't want Akeha to die."

"Akeha will not die. I promise you that. Help is coming."

"But they're going to take me away."

"Mokoya." The Head Abbot sighed as Akeha tried to turn their head, tried to look at the expressions on both their faces. "You won't have to go to the Tensorate alone. Akeha will go with you."

And Mokoya fell silent, even as their lungs worked rhythmically through their stress. Then: "You mean—"

"I cannot separate the two of you, Mokoya. That would clearly be an unthinkable cruelty. Your mother sent both of you here because of a deal we made. I have decided not to hold her to it."

Mokoya's voice shook with terror and hope. "So we'll go . . . together?"

"Yes."

"You promise?"

"Yes, Mokoya. Now help me with your sibling."

Mokoya twisted their fingers into Akeha's and started to sob again. The Head Abbot laid a second hand on Akeha's head. "You must relax, child. Sleep. You will be better when you wake."

His hands sent slowness and warmth throughout Akeha's consciousness. As they faded into the gentle cradle of sleep, they thought, *But you still look at me like I'm just a number in a column.*

PART TWO

THENNJAY

Chapter Six

YEAR SEVENTEEN

"**THE HEAD ABBOT** is going to die soon."

Akeha opened their eyes a slit. Mokoya lay on their divan across the room, silhouetted by the night sun that filtered through the thick paper pulled across the window. They considered pretending they hadn't heard it and letting that pronouncement die in the quiet night air.

Then reality settled in. Of course Mokoya would know they were awake. "Why do you say that?" they said, refusing to sit up from the bed.

"I saw the confirmation ceremony for the new one."

"Oh? Who was it?" Akeha lazily rotated the memories of the monastery's senior ranks through their mind. They hadn't thought much about those people in the time since they'd left, and suspected nothing much had changed in the nine years since. The monastery was a place of stagnation, a place that loved its doctrine and cared more about inner purity than anything else.

"No one we know. A young man."

"What?"

"Someone our age, maybe a bit older, maybe twenty."

A preposterous idea. It took twenty years for acolytes to complete their training, and from there it was a slow climb to the top. No one that young could take the post.

"A Gauri boy."

That was the thing that got Akeha to sit up. "A Gauri—are you sure you had a vision, and not a fever dream?"

Their twin sat up, and in the dark, they heard the click of a lid opening. Soft blue suffused the room as Mokoya prized the capture pearl out of its box with careful fingers. The glass drop, small enough to fit in their palm, glowed silver and aquamarine and plum with a freshly decanted vision.

Akeha had objected when the Tensorate's researchers presented Mokoya with the dream recorder. It seemed suspect that they wanted Mokoya to wear it all the time, even though the visions only happened in their sleep. The way Akeha saw it, it was just another way for Mother's lackeys to control Mokoya. But Mokoya seemed to appreciate its presence. And it turned out to have its uses.

"You can see for yourself," they said, holding it out.

The pearl harbored alarmingly lifelike warmth. Akeha tensed the vision open, unspooling its coils like a snake. Mokoya's vision washed over them.

A procession of monks sang sutras as they shuffled down the thoroughfare in front of the Great High Palace's ceremonial pavilion. Tensors and palace staff lined every building, every corridor, hands folded, watching silently. Handbells rang, rhythmic and solemn, and heads bowed as the front of the procession passed them by.

Leading the procession was a young man Akeha had never seen before. Lean and broad, dark-skinned, jaw framed by a hefty beard that seemed impossibly neat. His head had been shorn and tattooed with the sigils of the five natures. This was him. The new Head Abbot. He *was* a boy. And it *was* preposterous. He looked like a student dressed up in ceremonial robes for a play.

At five-step intervals, the new Head Abbot stopped and bowed, pressing his forehead to the ground. The boy's face was perfectly serious. Akeha watched as he got to his feet, walked five steps, and bowed again. Deep-set eyes, straight and narrow nose. He had a presence that could be felt even through the echo of a vision. And the vision lingered on him—in a way that Mokoya's visions never did—as if the fortunes, too, found him irresistible.

A Gauri boy. Extraordinary.

Where was Mother in all this? Akeha pulled on the reins of the vision and spun it around, searching for the Protector in this theater of ritualized obeisance. They'd learned to do this recently, based on notes they had *borrowed* from the laboratory studying Mokoya's visions. It turned out they weren't just dreams, but chunks of time captured in their entirety. With enough willpower, you could navigate through them.

Akeha found the Protector on the high dais in the ceremonial pavilion, shaded by awnings of yellow silk. Sonami was seated next to her, as she usually was these days. Kara, Sonami's youngest, clung to his mother's lap. He didn't look much older than he was now, freshly turned three and freshly declared to be a boy. Mokoya was right: this was going to happen soon.

Mother's face looked like she'd drunk a cupful of vinegar. Good.

Akeha exited the vision and pressed the pearl back into Mokoya's waiting palm. "Ha. Did you see? Mother's going to burst a vein."

"This isn't a joke, Keha. There's nothing funny about it."

Akeha quieted. It was crass, they supposed, to be amused by this turn of events. The Head Abbot's health had been failing for several years, but the old man had looked after them as children. He was the closest thing they had to a father. "I'm sorry."

Mokoya sloshed the vision around in their hands. "I don't understand," they said finally. "Why him? Who is he?"

"It's the flow of fortune. Why start questioning it now?"

The capture pearl froze sharply midrotation. "Why don't you ever take anything seriously?"

Akeha blinked. Their twin shoved the pearl back into its box, closing the lid with a harsh snap. "Moko," they said appeasingly, but it wasn't enough to stop them from furiously collapsing back against the divan.

"Oi." Akeha slipped off their own bed, hesitantly, afraid to cross the gulf between the furniture. They half stood, half leaned against the hard wood of the bed frame. "What's the matter?"

"Nothing," Mokoya said. They had turned to face the wall. "Go back to sleep."

Akeha sucked on their bottom lip and let several seconds pass. When Mokoya said nothing further, they ventured, "It's not nothing. You've been grouchy for the last few days. Something is wrong, you just won't say it."

Silence from the other side of the room. Then Mokoya sat up, slowly. "Our birthday is in less than two weeks. I want to be confirmed."

Akeha sucked air between their teeth, willing what

they'd just heard to change. "What?"

Mokoya turned. "I want to be conf—"

"I heard you. *Why?*"

"Why? Keha, we're turning seventeen. We have to do it at some point."

"We made a promise never to get confirmed."

"We were *six* when we made that promise. We're not children anymore." Mokoya shifted on the bed. "Keha, you didn't really think we could avoid confirmation forever, did you?"

Akeha shrugged, not trusting their mouth to say the right things. Nobody jumped from undeclared gender straight to confirmation. They'd take a couple of years to be sure. Unless they were Sonami, and Akeha wasn't Sonami.

Mokoya sighed noisily. "Keha."

"So that's why you didn't talk to me? You thought I'd be upset?"

"Well, you are."

Akeha wordlessly clambered back into bed. *I'm not upset,* they thought. *This is not a big matter.* But it was.

"You don't have to decide now if you don't want to," Mokoya said. "I'm just telling you that I'm doing it."

Akeha lay motionless on the divan, which suddenly seemed unreasonably hard and lumpy. They watched spots of light dance across the ceiling and listened to the uneven cadence of Mokoya's breathing from the other end of the room.

Eventually Akeha asked, "And what will you be confirmed as?" But even as the question left their lips, they already knew what the answer would be.

"A woman," Mokoya said, without hesitation.

The room was silent except for the soft sounds of their breaths.

Into the dark their twin repeated, "You don't have to decide now. I'm just telling you what I want."

~

The sun beat down upon baked dirt and brick as the twins slipped through Chengbee's intestinal byways like fish, flat-soled feet barely making a sound as they ran with the shadow of the Great High Palace at their backs. They had shed the company of their hapless minder, Qiwu, long minutes ago, losing him in the thick porridge of the main market's morning crowds. Now they were putting distance between themselves and the places they were meant to be. Mokoya, racing slightly ahead, traced the twins a solid path through the twisting streets.

They were headed south, to the ragbone-meat quarter. Mokoya's pace slowed as they headed into unfamiliar territory, trying to connect real living streets, in all their dirty, shouting confusion, to lines on a painted map.

The ragbone-meat quarter had its own market, a gregarious collection of carts assembled at the confluence of several streets. Unlike the main market square, with its artfully arranged displays and slackcraft-powered signage, the ragbone market pulsed with barely contained chaos. Rolls of dried goods flanked battalions of preserves heaped upon trays. Craftswomen rubbed elbows with men selling candied nuts in paper cones. Children in assorted shades of brown darted to and fro, hawking pots of spiced tea and fruit on sticks. Laundry flapped in second-floor windows, soaking up the perfume of incense and hot oil and roasting chestnuts.

Looking at this bright and symphonic scene, someone from out of town—a traveling farmer who did not buy the news scrolls, perhaps—would never guess that just a few days ago, the ground they stood on had been glutted with sitting bodies, living and breathing, arms locked in protest, boldly facing down lines of Protectorate troops. The city's tiny Gauri minority was often characterized as hardworking and easy to please, but the past week had clearly shown that they had limits.

That limit was this: seventeen of their compatriots killed in a silk factory fire and the factory owner exonerated from blame, even though it was clear the fire had been the fault of his greed and carelessness. Minor riots had broken out before more calculating heads swept in and organized sit-ins. For days the arteries of Chengbee's southern quarters had been obstructed by clots of protesters, singing and obstinate, arresting the flow of commerce.

The Protector finally defused the situation by executing the factory owner. Official pronouncements declared the incident over, justice served, and harmony restored. But the acid stares of the crowd as the twins plowed through it told a different story. Even if the people did not recognize them, Mokoya and Akeha looked Kuanjin and wore clothes of fine quality. That was enough to draw their ire.

It was far from an inspiring endorsement of Mother's rule.

Mokoya reached into the fold of their robes and extracted a picture scroll. It was the same one they'd woken Akeha with in the morning, exclaiming, "I knew I'd seen him *somewhere!*" Rolled on its inner surface was a crisp light capture of the Gauri protesters: a row of calm, determined faces, most half bowed or eyes shut as if in prayer or meditation. The lone exception was a young man who had been looking right at the woman who had tensed the light capture into permanence. Frozen in a semifrown, he stared intensely, his mouth a disapproving, unyielding line. Their mysterious future abbot.

Mokoya scanned the crowd as they threaded through it, looking for easy targets. Most avoided their gaze, ducking their heads as they saw Mokoya, some less subtly than others. But one woman—a vendor of straw mats and slippers and other woven things—was too slow, and Mokoya caught her eye.

"Honored aunt," they said, approaching the woman respectfully, "could you tell me if you've seen this man?"

They showed the picture scroll to the woman. She waved her hand and made inaudible excuses.

Unfazed, Mokoya moved on. Akeha followed quietly in their wake. A strange, glacial distance had swelled between them, a kind of false peace, the tangles of arguments to come writhing under the surface. As Mokoya accosted passerby after passerby, Akeha watched the crowd instead. Watched the way people's movements changed in the orbit of their twin. Watched the way Mokoya deformed the world around them. Over the years, and perhaps by necessity, Akeha had learned the trick of sliding quietly into the background, drawing as little attention as possible. Very different from their twin.

So Akeha watched. And it was through watching that they noticed the old man who was watching back. He was a shoe mender, crouched on a stool under the sign advertising his services. Instead of fear or disdain, his expression was touched by something resembling hope. And that interested them.

They let space and bodies come between them and Mokoya. Casually, incrementally, Akeha walked up to the watching man.

Their eyes met, and Akeha nodded at him. The man didn't return the gesture, but he didn't look away either. He had the tanned skin and wide cheekbones of a southerner, the look of someone who lived farther downriver than Jixiang. And he wasn't as old as Akeha had thought. Just weathered.

"Busy day, uncle?" Akeha asked.

"As if." The man snorted. "If you think this is busy, you should have seen this street before all those troubles came." He gestured in front of him with hands that were blunted by his craft. "Normal days, I get four or five customers by morning. Today, nothing. It's been like this for a week. A man needs to eat, you know?"

"Of course. There's been a lot of trouble in this quarter lately. Were you here during the protests, uncle?"

"Where else would I go? I live here, I work here. Of course, those people don't care."

"That must be difficult." As the man huffed in agreement, Akeha said, "We're looking for somebody connected to the protests."

"Hah." The man slapped a thigh. "Hah! I knew you were Protectorate. One look, I knew."

It occurred to Akeha that recognition of the prophet child of the Protector might not be as widespread as they'd assumed. "We're not here for trouble. We just want to talk to someone."

"Which one of them? Hah, you know, they all look the same to me sometimes."

The man's laugh, Akeha decided, was markedly unpleasant. "A young man. Very tall, big beard. He sat in the front row at the protests."

"Oh, that one." The man muttered something inaudible, shook his head, and gestured. "Go to the circus. Behind, over there. Ask for the doctor."

Akeha looked where the man pointed. Their mind turned this information over and over. *A doctor?*

"Thank you for your help, uncle." The monastery had taught Akeha to express gratitude for favors granted, no matter what unpalatable form the favor came in.

They caught up with their twin. Mokoya had cornered a woman selling jars of pickled vegetables and was on the verge of convincing her to give them directions to the circus. But the woman looked up, saw Akeha approaching like a shark, and changed her mind, waving Mokoya off with a muttered excuse.

"Honored aunt, it's really important," Mokoya said. "The future of this land could depend on it."

The woman stared blankly at them.

"Come on, Moko," Akeha said. "I've found out where he is."

Mokoya narrowed their eyes. "How?"

"Talked to an awful old uncle. Come on."

Mokoya fell behind in the viscous crowd, a half dozen steps' worth of reluctance between them. Akeha slowed until they were both abreast. "Are you all right?"

"I am." Mokoya squeezed their hand once, quickly and tightly. "Thank you for coming here with me."

"Why are you thanking me?" The idea of Mokoya sneaking out alone was unthinkable. "Who else is going to take care of you if you get into trouble?"

Mokoya punched them lightly in the arm. A couple of loping steps later, they said, "I thought you were still angry with me."

"I wasn't angry."

Mokoya glanced sideways at them, and a small smile tweaked the corners of their lips.

Conversation lapsed into pensive silence. As the clamor of the market subsided into the burble of a busy street, Akeha said, "So how come you decided to be a woman?"

Mokoya's puzzled frown revealed everything they thought about this question. "I didn't decide anything. I've always felt like one. A girl."

"I see."

"Don't you?"

"I've never thought much about it," Akeha said slowly, which was only slightly skirting the truth. Ideas and feelings bubbled as though their mind were boiling over. None of it lined up into coherent, defensible thought.

"You'll figure it out, anyway," Mokoya said with a confidence that ended where Akeha began. They nodded to their twin, as silence took up its easy crown for the rest of the walk.

~

The circus nestled on the borders of the ragbone-meat and paupers' quarters, in the courtyard of a disused tanning factory. Its rotting timbers and shingles formed a stern backdrop to the dozens of horse-drawn carts arranged in a loose semicircle. Circular tents of plain waxed cotton had sprung up in between them. Some had laundry hanging outside, others racks of drying fish. Along one side of the main clearing, rows of weathered benches sat under hand-erected awnings. Once, long ago, this had been a traveling circus, but weeds had grown amongst the wheels, and mold speckled the sides of the tents. Chickens pecked in the dirt, and a pot of curry simmered somewhere close by.

The eerie silence reminded Akeha of a plague ward,

but suspicious eyes watched them from slits in the fabric of the tents. The only other signs of human life were a couple of rail-thin children who had been kicking a rattan ball around. They stopped and stared sullenly as Mokoya approached.

"We're looking for the doctor," Mokoya said.

The younger child—a boy—ducked behind the other one, a girl bearing an ironclad expression. She pointed wordlessly to one of the tents, never taking her large dark eyes off Mokoya.

The twins turned in the direction the girl had indicated. Behind them, the children burst into a smatter of furious whispers, a collision of words in their own language. Akeha did not blame them for being intimidated.

The tent's roll-up door was closed. Mokoya pulled the heavy canvas aside and stepped in, Akeha right behind them. "Hello?"

A tall boy stood with his back to them, wrapped in patterned crimson cloth that left half his torso bare. He was sorting through an army of powder bottles on a cluttered, dye-stained table and didn't look up. "The clinic only opens on water and metal days. Come back tomorrow."

"I'm not here for treatment," Mokoya said.

The boy turned around. His face, those eyes, were exactly as they had been in the light capture. In person, he seemed both more normal, and more intense than in the picture. And he was much taller than Akeha had imagined.

He was beautiful.

The boy's expression changed as his gaze swept over the twins. Here was someone, at least, who recognized who they were.

"I have something to tell you," Mokoya said.

Chapter Seven

HIS NAME WAS Thennjay Satyaparathnam. He had just turned nineteen, and he was a healer by day and a storyteller by night. His role as a nexus of protest was mostly an accident. Mostly.

"So this was what that Tensor was doing," Thennjay said. He had the picture scroll stretched between his curious hands and was turning it this way and that under the glare of a suspended sunball, as if the light might reveal something of its inner workings. "She showed up at the protest with this strange wooden box, and she kept pointing it at us. I thought it was a weapon." His laugh bubbled up from the belly. "I realized it wasn't one when nobody died. When the Protectorate wants blood, it doesn't usually hesitate or fail."

The three of them were cross-legged on the floor of the tent. Akeha took another sip from the cup cradled in their palms. The liquid rolled in their mouth: spiced tea so laden with sugar and ginger it went down like a punch. Thennjay rolled up the picture with deft fingers and handed it back to Mokoya. "How does it work?"

"It's slackcraft," Mokoya said, slowly. "I'm not sure I could explain it to you if you're not familiar with the five natures." And then more quickly: "Not that there's anything wrong with that—it's just that it's complicated."

Akeha was not used to watching their twin speak this delicately, putting down words as if they were stacking porcelain cups.

Thennjay folded his hands in his lap. "I know a bit of the theory. You can try me."

"Light," Mokoya said, "has connections to metal-nature, for reasons we don't fully understand yet. You can re-create a scene, the colors and everything, by copying the shape of metal-nature in a box and bringing it back to artisans in the Tensorate, who then paint what they see."

"This is remarkably lifelike for a painting." Thennjay reappropriated the scroll, put it next to his face, and imitated his own expression.

Mokoya ducked their head to hide a smile. "The artisans are very good."

Thennjay had grown up on the margins of Chengbee, several generations removed from Antam Gaur. His father had been a fire breather and a storyteller; his mother a stilt walker and a doctor. In the circus, everyone took on multiple roles. Everybody did what they could. The line between community and family was thin and blurred here. When Thennjay was five, his father was among sixteen circus members arrested for putting on a series of farces, slapstick satire deemed to be insulting to the Protector. The charges laid were sedition, and the sixteen had been exiled south to perform hard labor, never to be heard from again. Thennjay's mother had then raised him until she died of a fever when he was eleven. Then the task had fallen to the rest of the circus, much as it was able.

The boy leaned back against his table. "So what are we going to do about this prophecy, then?"

"Nothing at all," Mokoya said. "There isn't anything we *can* do."

Puzzlement marred his face. Mokoya explained, "We've never been able to change the prophecies, no matter what we've tried."

"*We*, meaning . . ."

"The Protectorate. Well, my mother, to be exact."

"What, do you mean she doesn't control fortune and the heavens, as they would have us believe?"

"Stop." Mokoya smacked him on the knee as he laughed. They moved with a simple, alarming ease.

"Surely it can't be that hard. You could just have me assassinated, for example. Then the prophecy doesn't come true."

"An assassination would fail. My mother has tried it, in the past. Not on you, but on someone she didn't want getting a position I prophesied."

"Of course she would."

"It backfired. Not only did the person get the position, they had enough blackmail material to ensure it would be a *hereditary* position. For nine generations."

"Quite a feat." Thennjay laughed until a thought occurred to him: "Wait. Are you saying that until your prophecy comes true, nothing can happen to me? That I'm fireproof?"

"No, I—" Mokoya halted. As the boy continued laughing, they hissed, "That is not what I wanted you to think!"

Akeha put their empty cup of tea on the floor and watched as Mokoya twisted into a coil of anxiety. "I'm not joking!"

The deep rumble of the boy's laugh was like a thunderstorm in the distance, which could sound comforting to some and be a warning to others. "Well, I was. I'm sorry."

Akeha studied the way the boy looked at Mokoya, an alien and gentle expression on his face. Was this what tenderness looked like?

Mokoya, completely oblivious, had their hands in their lap, staring down at the lightly curled fingers. "It's best if we don't interfere with the prophecies. Nothing good has ever come of trying to change them."

Thennjay frowned. "Then why did you come here? To warn me?"

"I . . ." Akeha could almost feel Mokoya turning the question over in their mind, slowly and carefully, like a grilled fish. "I was curious about you. Wouldn't you do the same thing, in my position?"

"I suppose."

Thennjay folded his hands together, mirroring Mokoya's pose, seguing into contemplative silence. Eventually, his gaze fell on Akeha. "You don't say much, do you?"

Akeha stared evenly back at him. "No."

The moment of silence stretched. Mokoya broke in: "This news must come as a shock to you."

Thennjay chuckled and sighed, and for the briefest moment, Akeha caught a glimpse of darkness lurking under the bright, easygoing exterior. "It is what it is. As you said, there's nothing we can do to change it, can we?"

"In the monastery," Mokoya said, "they taught us that fortune is both intractable and impartial. That when bad things happen, it's the result of an incomprehensible and inhuman universe working as it does. The mountain shrugs, but thinks nothing of the houses crushed in the avalanche. That was not its purpose."

"And that's meant to be comforting?"

"Yes," said Mokoya, a little too earnestly. "Because it's not about you, or what you've done. There's no bigger reason to things."

Thennjay stared at the heavy canvas ceiling in contemplation. Then he said, "Growing up, I was taught to believe that the fortunes don't give you more than you can handle. It was a mantra, almost. Something bad happens? Well, you can handle it, because otherwise why would it have happened? I think it was the only way people could cope with the things that went on, sometimes."

"You don't sound like you agree."

He looked in the direction of the tent door. Heartbeats passed. "You saw Anjal and Kirpa," he said. The suspicious children outside. "They're six and four. Think about that, six and four. Their parents died in that factory fire. They don't have surviving close relatives. No grandparents, no aunts or uncles. A cousin is looking after them, but he's got hungry children of his own to feed. I ask you: Can you believe, *really* believe, that they're supposed to have the strength to cope with that?" He shook his head. "My personal belief? I don't care about the fortunes. I care about doing whatever you can, with whatever's in front of you. Because it's the only thing you *can* do."

Mokoya stared at him with a mixture of joy and disbelief, like he was some sort of miracle. "That's beautiful."

A feeling like a fist pressed against Akeha's sternum.

Thennjay turned to Akeha. "And you, what do you believe?"

Akeha leaned back, balancing on their tailbone and

clenched hands. "Why do my beliefs matter? I'm not a prophet or a future abbot."

Mokoya swung around with a furious glare. *Keha, what?*

Akeha barely blinked. *We've been gone a long time. There's going to be trouble.*

Mokoya's nostrils flared. But of course Akeha was right. They turned back to Thennjay, defeated. "We need to go. We sneaked out of the Great High Palace, and Mother isn't going to be pleased."

"Starting my career in the disfavor of the Protector? That sounds dangerous." The boy got to his feet, and offered a hand to Mokoya. After a brief moment of hesitation, they took it.

"I don't know what's going to happen next," Mokoya said. "What steps Mother is going to take, or the Grand Monastery. Once word spreads, people are going to start coming to see you. I'm sure of it."

He would be the most unqualified candidate for Head Abbot in the history of the Grand Monastery, Akeha thought uncharitably. Could he even perform basic slackcraft?

"We'll cross that valley when we reach its borders," Thennjay said. He still hadn't let go of Mokoya's hand.

Mokoya wasn't pulling away, either. They were staring up at Thennjay, at his face, at his broad-shouldered bulk.

"If you could stand to escape the palace again," Thenn-jay said, "you should come to the circus tonight. We put on quite a show, and it's only five brass tals per entry."

"I . . ." Mokoya lowered their hand slowly as Thennjay released it. "I'll try. It's not easy to leave the Palace without being noticed."

Thennjay smiled, an expression radiant as a firework. The two of them were standing so close to each other their bodies nearly touched. The boy said, "I have a feeling we'll meet again soon, my dear prophet."

~

Akeha's feet kicked up dust as they cut through the rumbling guts of Chengbee. The aftertaste of ginger tea clung pungent and sticky as glue to their tongue and mouth. Mokoya might have felt the same way, all wrapped up in a thick, woolly layer of thought. Akeha watched the back of their head, the black peach fuzz emerging from it, and thought about the long years they'd spent shaving their heads like they were still acolytes, so that they could appear identical.

They conjured an image of what Mokoya might look like as a woman, silk-draped and pigment-smeared, hair wrapped into unnatural shapes. This woman, this stranger, laughed with painted lips and clung to the arm of the tall, handsome man who smiled approvingly down at her. She made trite jokes and used the feminine version of "I." Akeha tried to imagine themselves in the same role: an alien form, making alien gestures. Their chest liquefied into molten ore.

"So," they said to their twin's silhouette, "is that why you want to be confirmed? So you can go around flirting with boys?"

Mokoya turned around, eyes as round as dumplings. "What?"

Akeha knew it was a bad idea, but continued talking anyway. "Come on. You saw the way he looked at you, didn't you?"

"What is *wrong* with you?" Mokoya hissed. They stormed a furious clutch of paces ahead, then slowed for Akeha to catch up. "You can be angry with me, but leave him out of it. He's got nothing to do with . . . whatever your problem is."

"He likes you."

"And you don't like him."

Akeha shrugged. "I don't have to. He's going to be the Head Abbot, not my new best friend." They snorted. "Unless I have to contend with him as a future brother-in-law?"

Mokoya's impenetrable silence only deepened as they turned away and continued walking. Furious. "You're going to the circus tonight, aren't you?" Akeha asked.

Their twin squared their shoulders, squared their jaw. "Fine. I am. I like him. I think he's important. *You,*" they added acidly, "don't have to come if you don't want to."

Chapter Eight

OF COURSE AKEHA WENT to the circus.

This time it was Mokoya who found the way out. A sympathetic gardener, an easily scalable wall, and a judicious use of slackcraft brought them to the city's ground level without being caught. After the fuss thrown about their morning escapades, it was almost too easy, Akeha thought. But they weren't about to complain.

The circus opened in the moon-half of the first night-cycle, and stretched into the sun-half of the second one. The audience numbered about a dozen, handfuls of Kuanjin and Gauri working class, chattering in their dialects, chewing through sweetmeats, greasing their fingers on fried dough sticks. Mokoya found seats in the front row, but Akeha chose to stand in the back, with a vantage over audience and performers both.

"Fine," Mokoya said. "Suit yourself."

The first act was a comedy duo, the usual bamboo-pole-soup-dumpling combination given a twist by comprising two middle-aged women in saris making jokes about sex and money, instead of two middle-aged men in robes making jokes about sex and money. Akeha scanned the crowd, the wings, the background. Thennjay was nowhere to be seen.

The comedy act was followed by an acrobatic troupe, earnest children who juggled heavy pots and flipped each other over a variety of stools and tables. Still no Thennjay. Akeha was used to being patient and staying very still, but irritated prickles flushed up their spine and raced across the skin of their neck. They pressed their teeth together.

Something odd caught their attention: in one of the back rows, a round-bellied man sat on the edge of the bench. He jiggled one leg relentlessly, bouncing his knee up and down, fingers drumming against his thigh. As Akeha watched, a tearful girl ran up: it was Anjal, the suspicious child from this morning. She grabbed the man's arm, bobbing up and down on her feet, and Akeha didn't need to know lip-reading or her language to understand that she was pleading for something.

The man wagged his head and shook her off. The girl hesitated, then ran off the way she came, still crying, clearly unsatisfied.

Strange. Where was her younger brother?

The lamps around the circus extinguished, plunging them into darkness. Akeha went rigid involuntarily and expanded their mindeye. The topography of living bodies lit up the Slack: audience, performers, constellations scattered around the tents of the living compound. These were the bright, simple stars of the common citizenry, borders whole and complete with few threads lashing them to the Slack—probably simple tricks they'd learned, mechanical spells to manipulate water-nature to help them with their work.

Then there was Mokoya, a comforting, blazing nova thick with embroidered filaments of light, solid cords of fibrous belonging stretching between them and Akeha. Through those connections Akeha sent a warning: *Be careful. Something's wrong.*

What is it?

I'm not sure. Just be careful. Keep your mindeye open.

Mokoya's star quivered with faint annoyance, but their presence sharpened into focus as they too opened their mindeye, shifting into the same plane of awareness as Akeha.

Then a third and unexpected presence appeared in the Slack.

The interloper glowed gently, his tapestry of Slack-connections not as complex as that of a fully trained Tensor, but still thick and thriving. Akeha recognized the intricate, furred edges into forest-nature that they often saw extending from the Tensorate's masters of biology.

Cheebye. They swore silently. How had they not realized? Thennjay was no simple healer, dispensing prayers and compressed mixtures of medicine. They called him a *doctor.*

He was a Tensor, or had been taught by one.

As Thennjay pulled at metal-nature, the lights came up around them: sun-strips, taped around the periphery of the circus, on the tent awnings, under the benches, wrapped around Thennjay's clothes. Akeha opened their eyes as the audience sighed in wonder. Thennjay held a tray of glowing spheres the size of ripe peaches, presumably part of his performance.

Akeha froze. The round-bellied man was gone. Empty space yawned on the bench where he had been. Where was he?

They spotted the man making his jittery way down the central aisle, toward Thennjay and Mokoya.

"Wait," Akeha said, straightening up from their slouch.

The man started walking faster. People stared. Akeha broke into a jog after him as Mokoya, in the front row, stood in confusion. "Stop!"

The man turned to face Akeha. Sweat picked out the terrified expression on his face, and then—

He detonated.

Akeha barely had time to throw up half a barrier, a shoddy one. It stopped the fire, but not the force of the explosion. Their spine met the ground with a sharp snap.

They scrambled to their feet, ignoring the pain that shot up their back. "Moko!" The air filled with screams, crackled with sulfuric fumes. Akeha's throat closed up, and their lungs heaved.

They smelled burning flesh. Akeha reached out and found Mokoya in the Slack, still luminous and steady. *Thank fortune.* They tensed through water-nature, dispersing black smoke so that they could see.

The man lay on the dirt, still alive, still groaning, meat crusted black and red. Clear fluid seeped through the cracks. Everything was blown in a perfect circle around him. Thennjay hovered over his doomed body, whispering urgently in their home language, holding the man's flesh and soul together through the Slack.

Mokoya ran to Thennjay's side, equal parts fear and anger. "What was that? What happened?"

Thennjay looked up at them, his splendid features hardened in anger. "Your mother," he said.

~

They weren't allowed into the tent with Thennjay and the dying man. Left outside, Mokoya smeared circular tracks into the packed dirt. As the sun rose into the second night-cycle, Akeha asked, "You didn't realize he was a Tensor either, did you?"

Mokoya glared at them, and continued pacing.

"You were distracted. He was so charming—"

"Shut up."

Akeha folded their arms and continued watching.

Mokoya made sixty-four more silent circuits before Thennjay stepped through the heavy canvas of the tent door. Sweat had collected on the front of his shirt, and blood stained his hands and clothes like cooking grease. He sighed with the weight of a thousand stones cast into water. "He's gone."

"That's a pity," Akeha said. The man might have been saved at a proper Tensor house of healing. The doctors, the masters of forest-nature, would have been able to reknit the shattered bones, rebuild the seared flesh. But Thennjay had said no. The community had said no. Akeha couldn't blame them for their distrust.

"You lied to me," Mokoya spat.

"I didn't," Thennjay said. "I said nothing. There's a difference. You never asked how much slackcraft I knew."

"You should have said you were a Tensor."

"I'm not." He kept his voice gentle. "The Tensorate and the Grand Monastery aren't the only ones who know slackcraft. My father had books. Scrolls. He hid them. After we lost him, my mother taught me as much as she could."

Mokoya's anger hissed between their teeth, in and out. "I trusted you."

Thennjay looked apologetic. "I didn't trust you." As Mokoya froze, the shock of this revelation wrestling across their face, he said, "I wanted to, I promise. But I couldn't. You're still the prophet. The Protector's child. And I'm just some troublemaking Gauri boy."

The anger went out of Mokoya: not a dissipation, but a deflation. Akeha almost felt sorry for their twin. The boy was charismatic, after all. Easy to fall for.

Akeha said, self-satisfied, "*I* never trusted you."

Thennjay spared them a glance, and in it was compassion, sadness, and a dozen other things Akeha couldn't parse. "That was the smart thing to do. After all that's happened this past week? I wouldn't trust me, either."

"You must think me a fool," Mokoya said softly, staring at the tracks they'd left in the ground.

"No." Thennjay lifted Mokoya's face by the chin, as something in Akeha's chest twisted. "You have a good heart. And that's a rare thing in these times. A beautiful thing."

Mokoya stepped away from him. "You smell of blood."

Thennjay quieted and then a muscle worked in his jaw. "They have Kirpa," he said. "Your Protectorate."

"What?" Mokoya looked at Akeha in alarm, then back at Thennjay. "Why?"

"The man in there. Jawal. He was their cousin, their guardian. Men snatched Kirpa from his sister's arms this afternoon. Then someone from the Protectorate came and told Jawal that if he wanted Kirpa returned unharmed, he had to do exactly what they said."

"To blow himself up?" Akeha frowned. "They asked him to sacrifice himself?"

"They told him, if you do this, all your children will be looked after. He's been struggling to feed them for so long. They knew how to convince him."

Ice and fire battled in Akeha's belly. A swathe of images clawed at them: shy Kirpa clinging to his older sister; Anjal's ferocity as she shielded him from strangers; the girl's tearstained face at the circus this evening. She was six years old. She had no business fearing for her little brother's life like that.

The twins must have been followed that morning, when they first found the circus. How could they not have realized? This was Mother at her best, brutal and efficient.

"Why would Mother do this?" Mokoya blurted. "She killed a man; she could have hurt us. Why?"

Thennjay shrugged, the movement like an earthquake. "She *wanted* you to be hurt, I think. Imagine how it would look. The Protector's children, maimed or killed after accepting an invitation from me? Even if she can't change the prophecy, that would destroy my reputation. I would have no power as a Head Abbot. There might even be war."

Mokoya seemed torn between incandescent rage and helpless tears. "It's awful," they gasped.

"It's *Mother*," Akeha rejoined.

Thennjay had already decided which side of fear or anger he fell on. "You know," he said softly, "I questioned your prophecy at first. I didn't know what role I could play in your monastery. But now your mother is trying to scare me. And I don't scare easily." He looked directly at Mokoya. "Take me to see her. We have some things to discuss."

Chapter Nine

"**HOW PRESUMPTUOUS OF YOU,**" the Protector said, "to think you can come to me with *demands,* as though we were equals. The audacity of it all. These are not the actions of someone fit for the abbothood."

The audience chamber of the Great High Palace had the quiet chill of a mausoleum and the emptiness of a mountain steppe. Slate and granite replaced the silk and wood the Protector preferred in her sanctuary, with massive gray columns holding the peaked roof high overhead. The three of them were mere pinpricks as they stood in the vastness in front of the Protector's dais, flanked by the stone-faced guards lining either side of the chamber. Thennjay was in front, Mokoya beside him, and behind them Akeha stood as an afterthought. They felt less unwelcome than ill-fitting, like a square of tile that was the wrong color.

"It seems that the fortunes have already weighed in on my fitness for the role," Thennjay said, his voice rolling with the depth of an avalanche. "Unless you wish to contest the prophecy?"

In contrast to their smallness, Mother lorded over everything on her high dais, magnified by the bright yellow of her robes. Her headdress glittered with the light of a hundred jewels, and sunballs suspended over the throne highlighted the sharpness of her cheekbones, the alpine slant of her mouth. Sonami stood behind her, calm and immovable as the stone pillars around them.

"I am aware of the prophecy," the Protector said. Her voice echoed off the floor and ceiling of the chamber. "I am also aware of its regrettable immutability."

She gazed unkindly down at the trio. "It leaves me no choice but to address the fact that a malcontent Gauri child born in an unnamed gutter has found an easy opportunity to latch on to power." She gestured with an operatic sweep. "Already your machinations have begun. I see how you have seduced my children to your side, even after the outrageous events last night." A predatory tilt of the head. "Know this, boy: I have no obligation to confirm your appointment to the Grand Monastery. My approval will come only with changes to the way the monastery operates. It has had far too much independence, for far too long."

Unfazed, Thennjay said, "You speak confidently for someone carrying so much sin. Your agents kidnapped an innocent child from my community. You blackmailed their guardian into carrying out a heinous attack that could have killed your own children. These are terrible things to have done. And it would be terrible if they came to light."

"What wild ideas you have." The Protector blinked lazily, like a satisfied predator. "Listen to you, trying to blame the reprobate nature of your people on me." Her teeth showed. "It seems the Gauri are good for nothing save violence and the spreading of falsehoods. I was very accommodating with your community over the matter of the factory fire. Perhaps I should reconsider that leniency."

"That's a lie," Mokoya exclaimed, their righteousness bursting forth at last. "He didn't do anything, and you know it. How can you command respect if—"

"Silence! How dare you speak to me of *respect*. After your disgraceful conduct yesterday, sneaking out of the palace like a thief, running around like some common criminal. Now you think to lecture me on how to command respect, when you can't even earn it for yourself?"

Mokoya stood silent, trembling, hands compressed into bloodless fists.

When Thennjay spoke, it was with the prickling, laden weight of air before a thunderstorm. "The philosopher Sadhya, a wise man, said that the powerful can make the truth dance to their song. That is why I brought my own recording."

The boy reached into the generous fold of his clothes. His hand emerged curled around a shiny black sphere the size of a plum, embroidered with blue lines of Slack charge. A tug through metal-nature set it humming. The hum turned into a voice: rasping and faltering, the last words of a man speaking a language Akeha did not understand.

"I spoke to your man Jawal before he died. His story contradicts everything you've said. It would be quite scandalous if people were to hear of it." He paused to let the implications sink in, like dye in a vat of water. When the Protector's expression was sufficiently dismayed, he said, "I want Kirpa returned to us unharmed. Reparations must be made to the family. After that, we can discuss the terms of my ascension to the Grand Monastery."

"Very bold," Mother said. She tilted her head. "Do you really think you can threaten me with one insignificant recording?"

"Are you willing to risk it? You know how restless we Gauri are. The last riots you had were years ago, and your soldiers were overwhelmed. You had to beg the Grand Monastery's pugilists for help. Can you bear more children for them? Or will it be grandchildren this time?"

Well done, Akeha thought. Thennjay had pushed Mother in ways they could only dream of. As a surge of genuine pride rose in them, they laughed into the ensuing, echoing silence.

Mokoya turned and fixed them with an acid glare.

Blood cooled in Akeha's belly. That single gesture outlined, in a dizzy rush, what they should have realized a long time ago: That in this, as with all things, they were expected to remain in the background, quiet and passive.

In defeat, Mother's face was a mask of deepest ice, pale and solid, betraying no trace of emotion whatsoever.

A clack of wood-on-tile echoed through the chamber. A familiar, rasping voice spoke up from the back: "Is this not something I should have a say in?"

Leaning heavily on a cane, Head Abbot Sung came shuffling up the interminable length of the chamber. He was a trembling, liver-spotted husk of the man Akeha remembered, but there was still enough pride and dignity left in him to face the Protector with bright eyes. Age had yet to diminish his mind.

"Master Sung," the Protector said, pleasantly enough. Was it Akeha's imagination, or was Sonami smiling behind her?

"Lady Sanao Hekate." The Head Abbot was old enough, bold enough to address Mother by her name. "If the boy's fitness for office is in doubt, the monastery has protocols, our ancient rituals, that can put them all to rest."

"No one is disputing that the Grand Monastery has its own criteria for appointing an abbot, Venerable One."

Mother's tone was perfectly civil.

"I am not opposed to the boy taking on the role. But if he is to do so, as prophesied, then he must pass the same trial that I, and all my predecessors, went through."

"The mountain trial?" Mother's lips curved into an imitation of a smile. "Of course. This is tradition, after all. And what is the Grand Monastery if not traditional?"

Thennjay looked to Mokoya. "What's the mountain trial?"

Akeha knew the answer to that. But the mountain trial was supposed to be mythical or allegorical. That was what the books in the monastery's library said.

The Head Abbot addressed him: "Do you know the name of the mountain that overlooks the city, boy?"

"Golden Phoenix Mountain," Thennjay answered, with slight suspicion.

"Do you know why it is so named?"

Thennjay frowned. His confidence, Akeha realized, came from preparation, and this unexpected questioning unsettled him. "According to legend . . . a golden phoenix led a band of starving villagers fleeing a war to safety. It guided them to this valley and flew into the mountains to nest. They built a settlement that became Chengbee and named the mountain after their savior. That's the legend."

"Legends form around grains of truth," the Head Abbot said. "To prove your worth as my successor, you must go into the mountains, seek out the golden phoenix, and return with two feathers."

Thennjay's face folded into a squint. "*That's* the mountain trial?"

The Head Abbot nodded.

Thennjay looked to Mokoya for reassurance, but their twin could only shrug helplessly. Was the Head Abbot serious? Who knew. He had ascended to the position nearly forty years ago. No one spoke of this at the Grand Monastery. It was a very practical place, and practicality did not encompass talk of giant, mythical birds.

It was a convenient way for Mother to save face, though, allowing her to cede the appointment of the Head Abbot to the monastery. She didn't have to admit that she had been outsmarted by a nineteen-year-old Gauri boy.

"Fine," Thennjay said, as if he had any other choice. "I'll do it."

Chapter Ten

"**YOU CAN'T JUST** *say* those things to Mother," Mokoya hissed at Thennjay. "You offended her. She'll remember."

"Good," Thennjay said. "I *want* her to remember." At this pronouncement, Mokoya's face tautened with a mix of anger and worry. Thennjay laughed, but not unkindly. "I want her to remember that I can be a serious threat."

They were corralled in the room assigned to Thennjay, a disused storage space in the servants' sector, barely larger than a clothes box. In a spurt of generosity, Mother had arranged for the provision of a single sleeping roll, which Akeha now sat lotus-legged on, watching the other two. Passively, as was expected of them.

The room was very small. Their legs and feet ached with inaction.

"You *don't* want her to remember." Mokoya turned away and paced as big a circle as the room would allow. "You don't know Mother. You don't want to be caught on the other end of her grudges."

Thennjay chuckled again, but this time there was weight in that sound, a history of stones and chains.

"Nao. I'm Gauri. I think I know a *little* about living under the Protector's grudges." As Mokoya's face wrinkled further, he said, "You don't think I'm taking this seriously?"

Mokoya burst at the seams. "Thenn, why can't you see that I'm worried about you?"

"Ai." Thennjay took hold of Mokoya's hands, held them gently. "I know."

Mokoya froze at the contact, but only for a moment. Thennjay continued, "Don't worry about me. It's going to be all right, I promise."

"So many things could go wrong," Mokoya said. "Outside the prophecy. You don't even know."

"I'm not afraid. I trust in the fortunes. What is your mother, stacked up against such awesome forces? Only a mortal, like the rest of us."

Watching them, Akeha's lungs filled with pressure, as if the air had nowhere to go.

"I've decided," Mokoya said, straightening up, eyes bright and hard as jewels. "After my confirmation, I'm not applying to the Tensorate academy. I want to return to the Grand Monastery." They tightened their fingers around Thennjay's. "Mother can't stop me. I'll be twenty-one in a few years, an adult."

"It won't be the same place you grew up," Thennjay warned. "After all, I'll be in charge."

"I know. And you'll need help. The old monks aren't

going to accept change easily."

Thennjay said, in his low, smooth baritone, "I'll be glad to have you there."

He had leaned in, closing the gap between his body and Mokoya's. Akeha already knew where this was going. It came from a playbook older than the Protectorate, older than human civilization. The confines of the room felt heavy, felt like prison walls.

A smirk cracked through Mokoya's seriousness. "I thought you didn't trust me."

Thennjay wrinkled his nose. "I guess I'm another big fool."

He moved forward, toward Mokoya's face. Akeha stood. The other two looked up in surprise, their small moment broken. It was as if they had forgotten Akeha was there.

"I'm going for a walk," they announced. And they turned to leave, ignoring the small mewl of "Keha?" that sounded behind them.

~

Akeha walked, deliberately putting one foot ahead of the other, pointed in a direction they weren't sure of. The Great High Palace was vast enough that they could wander for days and never recross the paths they trod. Their ambulation took them far from the servants' quarters, deep into the diplomatic wing. Puddles of yellow light punctured the night darkness, infrequently broken by the passing shadows of palace staff, working deep into unsociable hours. One of them—an assistant to Diplomatic Minister Kinami—smiled patronizingly at Akeha as she passed by. "Wandering about without your twin?" As if she couldn't imagine that Akeha had desires of their own, a mind of their own. They didn't reply.

Akeha usually delighted in the night halves of night-cycles. Not because they were darker than the night halves of day-cycles—they weren't—but because of the solitude they offered: the quiet corridors, the night song of crickets, the masses slumbering in their chambers. But tonight the solitude felt less like a warm cloak and more like a blanket pressed over the nose and the mouth. Thoughts thrashed through Akeha's mind like dying fish, and like fish they slipped away the moment Akeha tried to focus on them. Instead a parade of images slithered by: a burnt, bloodied man. A girl's face wet with tears. Mother's icy, restrained rage. Things that they'd idly stood by and watched happen.

But even as they chased these piscine threads of thought, they knew that a shadowy epiphany, full of teeth and eyes, stalked behind them. They didn't want to look at it. Didn't want to think about it.

Back in the room, with Thennjay, Mokoya had slipped and used the feminine "I" pronoun.

It shouldn't have bothered Akeha as much as it did. Mokoya's choices were their own. Yet it felt like their twin was pulling away from them, standing at the prow of a ship headed into uncharted waters where Akeha could not follow.

Akeha walked and walked.

The diplomatic wing had a courtyard of its own, an austere stone garden with an enormous black plinth standing in its middle. The plinth was a work of art, titled *Reflections upon the Past and the Future.* Its ebony surface was polished to glasslike smoothness and lit by a dozen sunballs fixed to the ground. Standing in front of its massive bulk, Akeha's reflection was superimposed over a void so pure and deep it seemed unending.

Akeha stared at themselves: the shorn head, the genderless robes, the stark facial features that were identical to Mokoya's. Until a young person confirmed their gender, the masters of forest-nature kept the markers of adulthood at bay. They had never imagined themselves any other way. It frightened them to think that this was not true for Mokoya. A fundamental chasm had opened between them, through which many other things could slip.

Their inner voice whispered, conspiratorially, *But that*

chasm's always been there. You've always known it, Akeha.

They stared unblinking at their own face as they recited feminine pronouns like a sutra. *I am. I want. I will.* And like a sutra, the words came out of their mouth rote and meaningless. There was no connection between what was said and the person in the black mirror.

Akeha bit their lip. A thought occurred to them. In all honesty, it had been occurring to them for some time, and occurring with much greater frequency since Mokoya's announcement two nights ago. It was a thought that took hold in the back of their mind whenever they looked at Thennjay, at the shape of his body underneath his clothes. A thought they had been trying to drown out, to ignore.

Slowly, as if stepping into the unilluminated edge of a lake, Akeha switched to using masculine pronouns.

I am. I want. I will.

Their heart quickened in their chest. The words rolled and clicked in their mind, sharp and electric.

I want. I want. I want.

Akeha had not grown up amongst men. There were male monks, to be sure, but they were not men as Kuanjin society considered men. There were no men in the Protector's family, and few amongst those she allowed close to her. Men were creatures of distant fascination, with their broad backs and tanned cheeks, and Akeha had never considered that they might be one of them.

They imagined themselves dressing like a man, with their hair tied up like a man. It felt different. Not *right*, exactly, but there was something there.

I want. I want.

I am.

Akeha's limbs trembled with the rush of adrenaline. This was it, the answer they had been looking for, scrambling to find over the past few days, ever since Mokoya dropped her basket of secrets. A new horizon unfolded, shining with ten thousand unnamed stars. New possibilities, new understandings, new ways of being. They should have thought of this earlier. Why hadn't they thought of this earlier? It was like cutting themselves open and finding another creature living inside, nested in their blood and bones and guts. Fear and excitement seized them in equal parts. *I should tell Mother,* they thought. *He* thought.

Tell her before I change my mind.

~

Mother was in her sanctuary, contemplating the twined branches of cherry trees in the garden. Like Akeha, she was someone who hardly slept, and she preferred the company of one of her concubines when she did. Akeha approached her from the back, studying her silhouette. Looking at her, it was easy to imagine Mokoya in thirty years' time, sitting gracefully in a courtyard like this, silk dress cascading around her. Face identical to Mother's.

Far more difficult to imagine what the future held for him. If it held anything at all.

Akeha had spent the winding journey to the sanctuary softly chanting *I am, I am, I am,* trying to get used to the sound of it on their tongue, his tongue. Each utterance sent a shiver through him, until he, they, felt stuffed so full of anxiety they might take flight, earth-nature of the Slack losing its grip on him. They had blocked out all other thoughts, intrusive thoughts, distracting thoughts, by filling their mind with the cadence of *I am, I am, I am. I am.*

Faced with Mother now, courage deserted them, and they stood frozen several yields away from her, unable to speak.

Mother turned around and stared at them with the curious demeanor of a raptor. Her attention was like sunlight concentrated under curved glass. Akeha's skin burned, and sweat collected in the small of their back.

"You did not come all this way to stare mutely at me," Mother said.

"I want to be confirmed. Like Mokoya." His tongue failed him, slipping back to the easy groove of the pronouns they had used since they were able to talk.

"Of course you do."

Akeha sucked life-giving air into his lungs and focused his thoughts very precisely as he said aloud, using the right pronouns this time: "I want to be confirmed as a man."

Mother stared at him for an agonizing second. And then she burst into laughter.

Akeha stood where they were, reminding themselves to breathe. Breathe, or they would get dizzy, and their skin would catch on fire.

Mother smiled without showing teeth. As if she would ever do something so inelegant. "It has been a long time since I've had a son." She tilted her head. "To think that it would end up being you."

"Was this—" Akeha licked their lips, bringing moisture back into their mouth. "Was this unexpected of me?"

"Unexpected?" Mother laughed again. "How can it be unexpected, when I had harbored no expectations for you in the first place? You were no part of my plans, child."

Akeha bit his lip so hard he tasted metal in his mouth. With the lip throbbing, he asked: "Do you object to this?"

"Of course not. Why would I?" She folded one leg over the other. She seemed strangely relaxed, even cheerful. It was not what Akeha had expected. "This has been a day of delightful happenings," she said. "I was presented a worthy adversary in that Gauri boy, who will soon come to power to oppose me. And now the spare child has finally chosen his own path."

A tremble ran through Akeha.

Mother glanced up at the canopy of trees, lights shining across her face. "Despite everything, the fortunes find ways to surprise you. I look forward to the days to come."

Akeha breathed. And breathed. It was the only thing he could do. Keep breathing.

"Have you told your sister?" she asked.

My sister. Akeha exhaled. "No. I have not."

~

Akeha told Mokoya the next morning, on upper-forest day. "I will be confirmed as a man." It was said, it was done, there was no turning back.

His sister said nothing in return. She pretended she was not upset. But that night, as Akeha lay in bed as though sleeping, she left the room they shared and did not return until the next morning. He did not ask where she had been, letting his mind fill in the blanks. Forbidden visions came to him of her and Thennjay entwined in a collusion of sighs and gentle touches. The images refused to leave his mind, no matter how he tried to cast them out.

The same thing continued to happen over the next two nights.

On the third day, lower-fire day, Thennjay left for the trial, accompanied by a guide from the monastery who would leave him at the foot of the mountain. Akeha spent the following days meditating, in preparation for the changes he was about to undergo. Mind empty, body blank, free of all emotions and base desires. It was a struggle. He felt too soft, too malleable, as though the slightest pressure would melt him.

Mokoya still did not return to their shared room.

When she finally came back, it was lower-earth day, the fifth day since Thennjay left. As the sun rose for the second night-cycle she sat in front of Akeha, her legs folded under her, hands placed loosely in her lap. Akeha burned with questions for her, rude and forward questions fueled by vulgar curiosity: What was it like, to lie with him? Were his hands strong or gentle, did he smell of earthy perfumes, did his flesh tremble against hers? But he remained silent.

"I want to marry him," she said.

"You've just met him."

"I know. But I love him."

"Mother won't allow it."

"I don't care what she thinks."

"He's going to be a monk. They don't marry." Akeha tilted his head. "Unless you think he'll change the rules for you?"

Mokoya sucked in a breath, her brow crumpling into ridges. "I . . . no. He would not."

"But you want him to. And it'll probably happen, too. You're so *special*, things always go the right way for you."

She shakily got to her feet, teeth bared at Akeha. "I don't know why I came here," she snapped. He tried to apologize, regrets bubbling in his mouth, but it was too late. The wall of her back disappeared through the doorway and did not return.

The next day, Thennjay returned from the mountain, bearing two ornate feathers the length of his arm. They gleamed dully in the sunlight, warm and yellow, topped by a teardrop-shaped plume that shone in a thousand colors. When asked about the details of his journey, he merely smiled and shook his head, bound now by the Grand Monastery's tradition of secrets. He had completed the trial, and that was enough.

Mokoya met Thennjay at the entrance pavilion, pressing her hands into his as they spoke. Akeha watched them from a distance. Mokoya's face was turned away from him, the words her mouth was shaping hidden. He looked at the two of them and saw a perfect circle in which he had no place.

A thought had hounded Akeha since he spoke to Mother about his confirmation. As he watched his sister embrace the man she loved, the edges of that thought crystallized into a solid plan of action. He knew what he had to do.

It was upper-fire day, the start of the new week. The week of their seventeenth birthday. The week their lives would start anew.

Chapter Eleven

IN THE ROOM HE had called home for the last eight years, Akeha was packing. He had put together some clothes, simple toiletries, a few days' provisions, and enough money that he could be comfortable, but not so much that he might be robbed. He intended to travel south, where the winds remained mild and the snows did not come, so he didn't need winter clothing. And he had enough confirmation medicine to last him a month before he had to look for more.

His body ached. His reshaped hips felt loose where the confirmation doctors had shifted bone, and soreness coiled in flesh both old and new. The doctors had assured him that the discomfort was normal, part of his body learning to speak the new language it had been taught. In time it would forget it had known anything else. In time, he too would forget what it felt like not to have this body, not to have had this life.

It would just take time.

His chin itched with fresh growth, dark hairs pushing through the skin for the first time. He hadn't decided what to do with it yet. Growing a beard might help him slip through the northerly regions where the shape of his face was still familiar, framed on walls in the official portraits of the Protector's family. Or not. The doctors had called forth a thick mane of hair from his scalp, and it now sat on his head in a tight bun. He had decided that he would cut it short, in the style of southern men, once he was on the other side of the Mengsua Pass.

Akeha gathered the small bags he had assembled and started tying them into his sling.

A commotion of stampeding feet was the only warning he got before Mokoya burst through the door, breathless and flushed with anxiety. "Keha," she gasped, "Sonami said—"

She froze as she took in the scatter of his belongings, the debris that had not made it into his pack. Her eyes widened as she realized the truth. "You—you're leaving?"

Akeha tightened the knot on his sling. "I am." He had told Sonami last night, as a courtesy to the woman who had raised him in early childhood. He made her promise to keep the news from Mother until he had time to leave the city. But of course Sonami would tell his sister. She was crafty in that way.

It was no matter. Mokoya could not stop him from leaving.

His sister blocked the doorway, her expression tumbling into the valleys of desperation. "Keha, whatever I did, whatever I said, I'm sorry. Please, don't go."

"It's nothing you did. You have a place in this city, in the shape of things to come. I don't." Akeha pulled the sling over his chest, feeling its weight settle onto his shoulder. "And if I stay here, I never will. I have to go. I have to find my own place in the world."

"What do you mean? Your place is here, with me. Wasn't that what we said?" Her voice cracked. "We were born together, we stay together until we die."

He would not be frightened by the talk of death, or the glasslike fragility she was exposing. "Moko. To leave is my choice. Just as becoming a man was my choice." He came face-to-face with her, forcing his expression to remain as calm as possible. "Would you really keep me here against my will?"

She was visibly shaking, as though she might disintegrate at any moment. Emotions deeper than terror laced her words as she said, "Everything I've done, you've picked the opposite. You think there's something wrong with me, don't you?"

"Moko. No." Despair sank through his gut. He wanted to reach out to her, but he couldn't bear to touch her, afraid that the contact might shatter his resolve. "I can't explain what this is about, but it's not about you. You have a future here with Thennjay. I want you to be happy."

Mokoya folded as she began to cry, collapsing against the wall in grief. Akeha resisted the instant urge to catch her, to hold her up, as he had so many times before. That was someone else's privilege now.

She had left a gap in the doorway, one he could step through easily, like his heart was made of stone. "Forget about me," he said, as gently as he could. Did she hear? He wanted to say *I love you,* but he couldn't bring the syllables to his mouth. Instead, he settled for "May the fortunes keep you safe."

Mokoya didn't look up, didn't respond to his words. She just continued sobbing. Then Akeha was through the doorway, through the gauntlet, his feet carrying him away as fast as they could. Behind him, he heard Mokoya screaming his name. He forced himself to stare straight ahead. He would not look back. He would not cry.

~

The lonely moon rolled across the sky as Akeha flew. He leapt from peaked roof to peaked roof, a hundred yields per jump, soaring as a bird might, landing as a feather would. He had learned this in the Grand Monastery: pulling away earth-nature so that weight fell from him, pushing through water-nature so that each jump had the speed of a released arrow. The night air sang in his clothes, his hair, his ears.

Below him, Chengbee slumbered, its squares of light dimmed or extinguished. From this height, the city was a dense, absurd plaything, something that looked easy to crush. In between the houses and matchstick streets, people vanished from view. Stay high enough, and the city became mere map, a territory, lines drawn on the edge of a mountain.

Akeha came to the city's southern edge, where the rivers Tiegui and Siew Tiegui met, where the spines of ships jostled for space along the quays, where the fertile plains downriver stretched silver and gray. He stood on the roof of an inn that nestled against the riverbank and filled himself with the cool damp of summer. This was it. This was his point of exit. He intended to find a ship with space amongst the cargo belowdecks, space he could slot himself into, and wait. The ships sailed downriver with silks and paper and Slack-powered devices, and with them he would go, hopefully as far as Jixiang, where the pass through the mountains waited.

"Akeha."

He froze. He had been so consumed by his thoughts, so focused on damming up the rising waters of fear and despair, that he hadn't noticed he'd been followed.

He turned, feet choreographing balance on the narrow

beam of wood. The silhouette making its way across the roof of the inn left him breathless with recognition. Thennjay looked the same as on the day they had met him, somber and beautiful, rich skin shining in the moonlight. "What can I do to convince you to stay?" he asked in his gentle baritone.

"Nothing." Akeha licked the parched surface of his lips as Thennjay drew close enough for him to smell. "I've made my decision. I'm not turning back."

"Mokoya is devastated," he said, voice unhardened by spikes of judgment. "This is hard on her. You should reconsider."

"She'll cope," Akeha replied stiffly. "She won't be alone. She'll have you."

His eyes drew across Akeha's face slowly. "That's not how it works." He reached out and took Akeha's hand, pressing fingers into skin. "I want you to stay."

Akeha pulled his hand back. "I've made my choice," he said, but his tongue was thick in his mouth, and it was hard to push words out of his throat. His skin was strangely alive where Thennjay had touched it. The taller boy radiated heat: heat that he could taste, heat that he could swallow.

Their eyes met. And in that moment, Akeha realized exactly what it was he wanted, and that this was the last, only chance he was going to get.

He surged up, like a storm wave, and kissed Thennjay.

The boy's lips were firm, easily parted, tasting and smelling like earth and nectar, sticky and pungent. As their tongues met, Akeha drowned, senses overwhelmed by a hundred different things at once, intoxicating and indescribable. Time warped and became meaningless.

Hands pushed against the curve of his back, firm and warm. Akeha broke from the kiss and pulled away, limbs trembling. His chest hurt. "No."

Thennjay's expression was equal parts sorrow and resignation. "Akeha . . ."

He found words somehow. "Promise me you'll look after Mokoya. Promise me you'll keep her happy."

Thennjay looked like he was studying his face, trying to commit every line to memory. "I can't promise that. I can only try."

"That's good enough for me." He stepped away, out onto the edge of the roof. "She deserves to be happy."

"Write to me," Thennjay said. "Send me signs that you are well."

Akeha dipped his chin in a nod. Not a promise, but not a refusal either. He would think about it, later, when he had gotten away. The taste of the boy lingered in his mouth as he dropped down to the waterline, to where the river rushed in an unending outward torrent.

PART THREE

YONGCHEOW

Chapter Twelve

YEAR TWENTY-NINE

"**WELL?**"

The man held the device up to the lamp, squinting at the dull surface with its one engraved character, a clumsy groove. He was a heavyset Kuanjin fence with an old scar rippling across his face. Akeha did not know his name. Twenty more devices lay spread between them on unbound cloth, ready for inspection.

Sweat had gathered on the man's lip. He tugged crudely through metal-nature and the device came alive. The warehouse's air thickened as it dampened water-nature. The device was designed to hamper sound recorders: call it privacy baffling, or counterespionage, or whatever was convenient. Who the buyers were, Akeha did not know and did not care. His supplier was a praying mantis of a man he had met with in a narrow alley in Cinta Putri. Where he got the devices from, Akeha also did not care.

"Well?" he repeated.

The man grunted in assent and replaced the device amongst its brethren. The warehouse he chose was in a row long since abandoned, air thick with dust and choked with the smell of rotting grain. And quiet. That was the important thing.

Satisfied with his inspection, the man reached into his sleeve and tossed Akeha a small pouch. It landed in his hands with a solid metallic clunk. He looked inside and nodded.

In the distance someone screamed.

Akeha frowned. A street over, the Slack burst with flowers of activity. Tensors fighting, clumsy sledgehammer attacks that betrayed a lack of pugilistic training. He listened: shouts, in Kuanjinwei. At least three involved.

His buyer noticed. "Protectorate business," he said.

Akeha grimly tucked the pouch away as he continued to listen, to watch the Slack. The pattern clarified: three attackers, one defender. All Tensors.

"Don't get involved," said the buyer. Not a warning, just advice.

"Our business is done," Akeha said. He straightened up and walked away. Behind him, the man snorted in derision of Akeha's judgment.

The streets were dusky and silent enough that muffled shouting echoed. This part of Jixiang, a mercantile quarter, had been abandoned in the tides of changing fortunes. Warehouses sat with gaping mouths that could swallow thieves, smugglers, the poor, the desperate. Akeha crossed spaces briskly: the fighting had subsided into a fierce glow in the Slack. All four Tensors remained alive, clustered in one of the yawning derelicts.

Akeha stayed in the shadows by the warehouse's entrance, his footprint in the Slack light and practiced. Three soldiers woven up in the Protectorate's padded gray faced a gasping young man in civilian dress. Blood covered half his head, seeped through the front of his tunic. The soldiers stood in a fan: two flanking, the leader confronting the bleeding man with some kind of tube weapon.

"Tell me where it is, and this can end," said the soldier with the tube. A man. The weapon crackled as he smacked it in his hand.

"You can threaten me with pain or death. I'm not afraid. And I won't tell you—"

The weapon sang, and electricity struck. The young man screamed and fell to his knees. Chemical burn seared the air.

In the ringing silence, the young man struggled back upright. "I won't tell you anything."

Akeha carried a dozen flying daggers: tucked in his belt, around his arms, on the border of his calves. He was aware of their weight, their heft, and the speed at which he could hurl them in between heartbeats. He was aware of many things at that moment.

He hadn't been noticed. It was not too late to walk away.

But Mokoya wouldn't, he knew.

Akeha closed his eyes, slowed his breathing.

His blow fell through water-nature. A shockwave knocked all four men flat. Akeha moved. The first soldier to stand died with a blade between the eyes, skull shattered from the force of the impact. The second was hit in the throat and collapsed, choking on flesh and gristle.

The leader surged forward, grasping at the Slack in panic. His weapon snarled with energy. Too slow. Akeha closed his hand. Water-nature responded. Like a noose, it snapped around the man's neck. Bone disintegrated, flesh ruptured, and the man dropped like a slab of fish, blood pooling around the ruin.

Akeha exhaled. Red patterned the ground in chaotic gouts, but he remained clean. None of the soldiers moved again. The Slack settled into reservoir calm.

The wounded young man sat on the floor where he had fallen, eyes round, mouth a gaping circle. As Akeha stepped out of the shadows, he scrambled backward, terrified, whispering prayers as though faced with the devil himself.

Akeha walked up to him and wordlessly held out a hand.

The young man stared at it. Thoughts and emotions filtered visibly across his narrow face. When he reached the point of realizing death was not forthcoming, he crumpled to the ground in a heap and started to pray. Akeha had been around Katau Kebang long enough to recognize words of gratitude to the Almighty.

He allowed himself a sigh.

When the young man finished praying, he fixed his eyes on Akeha with surprising clarity. "Who are you?"

"A friend. We need to leave."

"Who sent you?"

He scowled, already regretting his involvement. "The fortunes."

"Was it Lady Han?"

"It was your Almighty," Akeha snapped. "Do you want to live or not?"

The man studied Akeha's face for a moment more, and his expression changed again. Suspicion had lodged there, along with a measure of curiosity. "You look like her."

"What?"

"The seer. You look like her. Are you—no, it can't be. Are you?"

Akeha took one breath in, let it out. Moved on. "You're

a Tensor, running from the Protectorate. You have something they want. I'm thinking these three goons won't be the last they send." He repeated, "Do you want to live or not?"

The man considered this, his brows knitted. His complexion was glazed with blood loss, and there was a telltale tremble to his limbs, an uncontrollable spasm of the fingers.

This time, when Akeha held out his hand, the young man took it.

~

His name was Yongcheow, and he had recently come from Chengbee. He didn't offer more, and Akeha didn't ask. The blood loss left him leaning his weight on Akeha. Something was wrong with one of his ankles.

The moon illuminated the streets of packed dirt before them, sides clotted with debris. The ghost quarters of Jixiang had been optimistically carved out of a hillside, then abandoned when they became too heavy a load to bear. The lights of the city proper glowed below them.

As they navigated toward the living streets of the city, Yongcheow said, "You never told me your name."

Akeha's vault of false names was large and easily

opened. It waited. He hesitated; an abyssal heartbeat passed. "It's Akeha."

"So I was right then. You *are* Sanao Akeha. The Protector's fugitive son."

Akeha didn't answer.

"Why did you save me?" Yongcheow asked.

"You looked like you were in trouble."

"I was. But you didn't have to step in. You don't know me, and I presume you weren't lying about not being sent by the Machinists."

Akeha frowned. He knew of the Machinists; he wanted nothing to do with them or their tendrils of rebellion. "You ask a lot of questions."

"I do. It's how I get into trouble."

They walked farther in silence. Yongcheow's steps had started to falter, each one heavier and slower. Akeha tightened his grip around the man's slender waist. "Keep walking," he said. On one hand, he was already braced to end the night burying another body. On the other, he really did not want to.

"You shouldn't have killed those men," Yongcheow said, breath clouding the air. His tone was gentle, not accusatory. It could have been from the blood loss.

"Would you have preferred I let them kill you?"

"Killing them wasn't the only solution."

"It was the least messy one." And he did not like to be reminded of it, even if it kept the young man conscious and talking. "Sympathy for them is how you got into trouble."

"You shouldn't have killed them," Yongcheow repeated, more softly.

Akeha did not respond.

As they started down the incline that would bring them into the parts of Jixiang that still lived, Yongcheow said, "Wait. Let's go down that alley, please."

The alley ended in a small grove of mountain dogwood, their short trunks twisted into ugly shapes. Yongcheow pulled away and stumbled magnetically toward one. Akeha followed closely, poised to catch him if something happened.

Gasping from the effort to stay focused, Yongcheow unstitched the bark of the tree where slackcraft had fused it over a hollow in the trunk. Concealed within was a cloth bundle. Unwrapped on the ground, it revealed several scrolls, a group of smaller bundles, and wooden treasure boxes. One of the boxes contained packets of powders and elixir drops. Yongcheow counted out a few of the latter and swallowed them.

Akeha studied the contents of the bundle. "Is this what they were looking for?"

Yongcheow nodded.

"And these." Akeha pushed at the nestling scrolls. "The Machinists' secrets?"

The man pressed a clumsy, urgent finger to Akeha's lips, as if he hadn't been on the constant lookout for soldiers following them. He flinched away in annoyance.

Still, in a burst of unearned trust, Yongcheow allowed Akeha to take custody of the cloth bundle. "My wounds are worse than I thought—" he began.

Akeha stopped him from finishing that thought. "I will help. But not here." He pulled Yongcheow to his feet. "Come. We've delayed enough."

Yongcheow swayed. "You're a good person," he said through soft lips, as Akeha held him firm.

Akeha looped an arm around him. "You'll regret saying that."

Chapter Thirteen

YONGCHEOW STAYED ON BOTH feet all the way to the eastern side of Jixiang, where the Flower Inn waited. The decorated yellow lanterns of the perfumed quarter lit the elbow-jostling street, where the passage of a bloodied man supported by another drew stares, but little comment.

Akeha wrestled his companion to the entrance of the inn, where they were met by the bulk of Ang, the inn's doorkeeper. He looked the two over, arms crossed, and warned, "No trouble."

"No trouble," Akeha replied.

Akeha was a regular at the Flower Inn, and Ang had known him for years. He grunted and stepped aside.

"Send someone up with water," Akeha said. "Two pails."

Ang nodded.

Yongcheow barely made it up two flights of stairs and down the wooden corridor to Akeha's room. Akeha released him onto the bed, where he remained seated, breathing very slowly. His clothes were heavy and stiff with drying blood. "Get undressed," Akeha said. He sought out his medicine cabinet.

"Wait," Yongcheow said. Akeha turned back, frowning. The other man pushed his hands against the hard surface of the bed to stay upright. "There's something . . . you need to know."

"What?"

"My confirmation, I didn't . . . I didn't get confirmed." As Akeha's frown deepened, he said, "I mean, I got confirmed, but I didn't go to the doctors. Some—"

"I don't care," Akeha said.

He turned away: there was work to do. Cloths for bandages, herbs and powders for salves, bowls to mix them with. Akeha's skill with forest-nature was self-taught and lacked the finesse to reknit a gash this deep. Needle and thread would help.

Broad-shouldered Amah was the one who brought the pails up. She glanced over at Yongcheow, his tunic off, compression bandages off, exposing a blood-thickened knife wound across the rib cage, and clucked. "Getting in trouble again?"

Akeha thanked her for the water.

"There's still soup left over from dinner," she said. "Do you want?"

He nodded. "Bring us two bowls later."

The wound had to be cleaned, disinfected, pulled shut.

Yongcheow leaned back, breath whistling through his teeth, as Akeha worked.

"So what is it you do?" he asked. "When you're not rescuing people in need."

Akeha threaded needle through flesh. "I'm a deliveryman."

"You're very good at killing people, for a deliveryman."

Akeha said nothing. The work before him required focus.

"So what do you deliver? And for whom?"

"Anything. Anyone. I don't ask. I don't look. I do the job. It makes everything simpler."

"Anyone?"

"No Protectorate. That's my only rule."

Yongcheow laughed, and Akeha halted as the man's side shook, the torn edges of the wound shifting. "You're a smuggler."

Akeha waited for him to still before returning to work. Black thread drew flesh to flesh, forest-nature set it on the path to healing.

Closing the wound was the easy part. The blood loss—that was harder to fix. A skilled doctor would have had ways to replenish the lost iron; Akeha was no such thing. He pressed the thick paste he had made over the gash, equal parts nourishment and antiseptic. Then he bound it with clean cloth.

"No compression until it heals," he said. The other man nodded.

The injuries clouding his head and legs were superficial, easier to deal with. Basic doctoring was simple; the rest was up to the fortunes.

Yongcheow's fingers grazed his chin. Akeha froze. "Thank you," the man whispered.

Akeha escaped the contact to prepare the strong, bitter healing brew.

His patient accepted the cup of dark liquid with a small expression of wonder. "Why did you save me?"

"We've discussed this."

"You didn't answer."

In irritation, Akeha turned away to clean the room. "Rest now. This place is safe. Soldiers won't find you tonight." And it was the best they could do for now. Tomorrow was tomorrow's affair.

~

Yongcheow slept easily; Akeha didn't. In a square of moonlight by the bed, soft as winter frost, he combed through the cloth bundle that had almost cost his companion his life.

The Machinist scrolls drew his attention first. They were lightning scrolls, new technology that had filtered south only in the last few months: thin sheets shaped out of lodestone paste, Slack-imprinted with information that required a decoder to extract. Their presence told stories—Tensor involvement, money, deep organization. In Akeha's line of work, he listened to a lot of talk. The talk about the growing Machinist rebellion in the capital said it was driven less by downtrodden farmers than by disaffected Tensors. Here was the proof, solid in his hands.

His companion, then: also one of those disaffected? The bundle told little of the man. The small wooden boxes held medicines, soaps, tools to mend broken things, money. There was a thin prayer mat, folded and rolled up. The third scroll was a copy of the Instructions, the holy edicts revered by the Obedient. An old copy, but well kept. Well loved. He looked for evidence of family, lovers, friends. Nothing.

Akeha unwrapped one of the last bundles. As he laid the cloth flat, its damning contents spilled into the light. Pearl-sized silver pellets. Blasting powder in packets, smelling of fireworks. And the main event, heavy and metallic, sitting in the middle of it all.

A gun.

Akeha had seen guns before. They were Tensors' playthings, put together by masters of earth- and water-nature for fun. The ones he'd seen used coiled springs and slackcraft and produced just enough force to punch holes in paper cutouts. This one was no plaything. It had heft. It had scars, black on the nozzle and stark across the body. It had a slot for blasting powder.

It was a weapon.

A weapon that didn't rely on slackcraft.

A weapon that didn't require a Tensor to charge it.

A weapon that anybody could use.

Akeha lifted it, felt its stonelike weight, put it back down. A slip of paper caught his attention. Unfolded, it revealed a scrawl of diagrams and instructions. Akeha recognized the signature appended to it. Midou. A friend from later childhood, a relative close enough to bear some prestige, a cousin distant enough to be dispensable. The paper was speckled with red that could be inkspill or bloodstain.

He rolled up the bundle, blood racing in his veins. If this was the Machinist endgame—arming the peasant masses with deadly weapons—then his understanding of the situation was broken and hollow.

Akeha looked over his shoulder. In the dark, on his bed, Yongcheow slumbered, pallid and inscrutable. A small man, caught up in a web of things beyond his ken. Akeha had to extricate himself before he, too, got caught in it.

Chapter Fourteen

YONGCHEOW WOKE AT FIRST sunrise to pray. Akeha, who'd slept on the floor, watched his slippered feet pad across the ground, pause to retrieve the prayer mat, then vanish behind a cabinet's bulk. He drifted back to sleep with Yongcheow's fluid supplications nestling in his ears.

Later, he woke again to a stirring in the Slack: Yongcheow pulling on fire-nature to dry freshly washed clothes. He sat up. The bed had been made, the cloth bundle reassembled. Yongcheow was half dressed, heating his tunic as it hung on a piece of string.

"What are you doing?"

"Oh. You're awake."

"Planning to leave before I woke?"

"No, I—" Yongcheow obscured his reaction in the flurry of putting on the tunic. "I need to get to Waiyi as fast as possible."

Akeha knew Waiyi. A foot-of-the-mountain hamlet in the wilds, several hundred yields off the river. It was surrounded by hills and good places to hide. He did a lot of business there. "I don't advise traveling. Your wounds need more time."

The stiff, cautious way Yongcheow fastened his tunic was proof he also knew this. "It's time I don't have. I would stay longer, if I could."

Akeha watched the man's face and movements intently as he posed the next question: "What are you carrying that can't wait one more day?"

"Information." He met Akeha's gaze head-on. "I know you looked through the bundle." When Akeha didn't deny this, he continued, "The information concealed on the scrolls is a matter of life and death."

"Information the Protectorate would kill for. What is it?"

Yongcheow's lips tightened. "Maybe . . . it might be better for you not to ask."

Akeha folded his arms and leaned against a wooden beam.

"It involves your sister."

Within him, Akeha's stomach lurched into movement. "Tell me."

A seismic sigh. "Your sister had a vision. She saw an attack on the Great High Palace by a small group of Tensors. These Tensors had connections to the Machinist movement. It's . . . complicated, and their motives were their own. But in short, the attack failed, and now your mother is purging suspected Machinists throughout the Protectorate."

"Purging . . ." Dread shivered through him. "Do you mean—"

"What do you think it means?"

Akeha looked to the ceiling, to where the rafters held firm. "How many dead?"

Yongcheow's shoulders tilted. "We can't save those in the capital. They got out, or they died. We're trying to warn everyone else. What I'm carrying are lists. A list of known members outside the capital, and a list of Protectorate targets. Not all the people on our list are Protectorate targets. And not all the people on the Protectorate's list are our people." He licked his lips. "We could save innocents by warning them."

Akeha closed his eyes and counted the stiff breaths that passed. When he opened his eyes, the world was still there. "What about the gun?"

Yongcheow remained mute for several heartbeats. Finally, he said thickly, "It was a gift. Bequeathed to me."

"I saw Midou's signature. He was a childhood friend."

Yongcheow's eyes were fixed on the air, on nothing. "He was a good man. Too good."

Silence bloomed. Yongcheow, regaining his composure, said, "In any case, now you understand my urgency."

Akeha said nothing. He had not been in the capital

in a long time. Mother's purges were stern, quiet things: doors pushed in at night, muffled bodies dragged from beds. Vanished. Mokoya once asked Sonami where they put all the graves. Sonami said, "Mother doesn't leave that kind of mess."

Yongcheow carefully tied the cloth bundle around himself, avoiding the wound. "Will you come with me?"

Akeha tightened his arms across his chest. "No Protectorate. That's the rule."

A medley of emotions ghosted through Yongcheow's face: disappointment, sadness, resignation, fear. "I see. Well . . . thank you for everything, then. His peace be with you." He stepped over the room's threshold.

"Wait," Akeha said.

Yongcheow swiveled as Akeha dove into a medicine cabinet. "Take these. You need to replenish your iron."

His fingers closed loosely around Akeha's as he accepted the elixirs. "Thank you." His hand lingered a moment longer than necessary, skin electric against skin. Then he stepped away, out of the room.

Akeha folded onto the unyielding surface of the bed, breathing very slowly. His thoughts turned briefly to Midou. Scrub-haired, knock-kneed Midou, who took everything with the gravity of a funeral director; Midou the gunmaker, Midou the unlikely rebel, Midou who was almost certainly dead. Strange to think of those familiar bones reduced to atoms, scattered across a hillside in Chengbee.

He shut his eyes, pressed cold fingertips to the bridge of his nose.

What would Mokoya do?

~

The fierce, shining ribbon of the river Tiegui broadened into sluggish green flats by the time it reached Jixiang, heavy with silt and soft at the banks. Diluted clumps of merchant ships bobbed listlessly in its eddies. When Akeha caught up with him, Yongcheow was walking the gray-skied docks, trying to find a willing oar among the merchants sailing upriver with the last of the harvest.

"Don't take the river route," he said. "It's too open."

Yongcheow had showed almost no surprise at Akeha's reappearance. "What's the alternative?"

"There's a path through the forest, along the buttress of the mountain range. It's longer, and shouldn't be traveled alone, but it'll be harder for soldiers to find you."

Yongcheow folded his hands behind him. "It sounds risky."

Akeha drew and released a full breath before speaking, knowing that there would be no turning back after this. "I'll take you."

A small smile spread from one corner of Yongcheow's lips to the other. "You changed your mind."

"Come," Akeha said irritably, "before I change it again."

Chapter Fifteen

THE ROUTE WOULD TAKE two days on foot. Yongcheow's injuries meant more precautions, fewer treacherous shortcuts. Over both day- and night-cycles they would travel during the sunup hours and rest during the sundown ones, taking turns to keep watch.

"You've done this many times before," Yongcheow observed.

"And you haven't. Not even once," Akeha replied.

He did not deny this.

In the monotony of light forest cover, routine settled upon them like a fisherman's net. They walked, they caught snatches of sleep, they walked again. This far south, at the periphery of summer and autumn, sunup and sundown hours matched each other in length. Light, dark, light, dark. Akeha trapped rabbits to skin and boil. Yongcheow sank into a fog of strange, serious contemplation, breaking it only to pray at every rest stop, and to answer questions.

Their first stop Akeha asked, "What has my sister said about the purge?"

"Who knows? She doesn't leave the monastery. You probably have a better idea of what she thinks than I do."

Their second stop Akeha asked, "Does she really not leave the monastery? Ever?"

"My friend, I'm half Kebangilan. My father is a provincial magistrate. Our village is so small people can't point to it on a map. I am—I was—no one in the Tensorate. Certainly not of the tier to hear the whispers that surround the Protector's family."

"I see."

Their third stop, Akeha said, "The gun. A Machinist initiative?"

This one drew a laugh, bitter as the frost. "If only! It was Midou's prototype for the Tensorate. In the end, he didn't want it in your mother's hands."

Steam rose in sheets from the pot of boiling rabbits. Clarity seeped into Akeha's mind. "The guns were for Protectorate soldiers."

"And Tensors. You must have noticed, most of us are useless at fighting. Get us a little nervous, and . . . that's the end of it."

"It just takes practice. Focus can be taught. Adrenaline can be a tool."

"Yes, Monastery-style training. That will go down well with the pampered brats stuffing the halls of the Tensorate academy."

"So, weapons, then. She must be preparing for something."

"Not necessarily. If she could arm Tensors, then she wouldn't need pugilists for close combat. You know she doesn't get along with the Grand Monastery these days."

"I know," he said. Pride swelled quietly at Thennjay's resistance to her rule.

"More than anything," Yongcheow admitted, hands tense around the cloth bundle he carried, "I'm afraid of Protectorate troops with these weapons."

"It's only a matter of time. If not Midou, someone else will perfect them."

"I know." The tendons in his hands stood out as he clenched them. Akeha resisted the urge to reach out and massage the stiffness out of them.

At their next stop Akeha said, "So, about you and Midou . . ."

Yongcheow's lowered lids occluded reams of history. "Many years ago, if that's what you're asking." At Akeha's patient silence, he sighed. "We were both in the academy at that time. He had recently converted to Obedience, and that's how we met. He was always a radical, agitating for change. I was afraid of what would happen to my family. So, we fell out."

"But you're here now."

Yongcheow pushed in the dirt with a broken branch.

"The Protectorate put his name on the list. I was added by association. They came for him first. He left me a warning, and—" He hefted the cloth bundle.

"Then you're not a Machinist."

"I wasn't. But I am now." He shifted his weight. "Don't misunderstand me, I'm not opposed to the philosophy. In fact, I agree completely. People should have access to technologies without relying on Tensors. I just didn't think I had it in me. Joining the movement, I mean."

"You underestimate yourself," Akeha said softly.

It was Yongcheow's turn to rest as the sun fell. In the soft shelter of willow crowns, Akeha watched shadows march across the warm canvas of the other man's face. As the patterns shifted and changed, he felt something in his chest come loose.

He spent the time between the third and fourth stops snarled in thoughts of possible futures. When they laid down their packs again, he ventured, "You didn't go to the confirmation doctors. Was that because of your religion?"

Yongcheow blinked. "That's . . . a very personal question."

"I apologize. I shouldn't have asked." He turned away to kindle damp leaves into flame. Under the ministrations of fire-nature, the detritus dried and crackled to life, the sound filling the damning silence. He watched the flames gyrate until his heart rate slowed, then he turned back. "I'm sorry."

Yongcheow met his gaze coolly. "It wasn't because of religion. Some Obedient don't alter their bodies because they believe we shouldn't touch what the Almighty bequeaths us. To me, confirmation doesn't fall into that. I just didn't do it because it didn't feel right for me."

Akeha nodded. "Thank you. I'm so—"

"Don't apologize again."

He nodded.

It was Akeha's turn to rest. He found a stone to sleep on and let dreams claim him with their wild trajectories. When three hours had passed, he woke to Yongcheow studying him with the same intensity he'd afforded the other man.

"You're the first son the Protector's had," he said.

"I am."

"It must have been a surprise for her."

Akeha laughed, a sound like pebbles rolling. He stood, brushing dirt away. "Everything about me was a surprise for her. My existence was a mistake."

"I don't believe that."

"I know, I know. The will of the Almighty."

Yongcheow exhaled. "Not just that. People make mistakes, they can't *be* mistakes. And I don't think you believe that either."

"Don't I?"

"If you do, then a mistake saved my life. I'm still grate-
ful."

Akeha snorted. He held out a hand, and Yongcheow
took it, pulling himself up.

The first day flowed over into the next. Their journey
relaxed into easier banter. Akeha pressed Yongcheow on
Machinist philosophy, a debate that rolled into a tangle
of points and counterpoints.

"No," Yongcheow said, exasperation creeping into his
voice, "we're not advocating the abolishment of *everything* that uses slackcraft. We just want to develop alter-
natives for laypeople."

"But you'll still need to rely on Tensors. As long as
there are things that can only be done through slackcraft—"

"We're not trying to abolish the Tensorate either! Of
course there will still be things that work on slackcraft—"

"Lots of things."

"Yes. Many. Like—"

"Talkers."

"Aha." Yongcheow brightened. "You'd be surprised.
There's been work done on this. Someone found a way to
record sounds as electrical signals, which you can trans-
mit instantly, or almost instantly, through wires."

"Wires."

"Yes. If you have devices connected by wires, you can talk."

"So if I'm in Cinta Putri, and I have someone in Chengbee I want to talk to, I have to run a wire from Cinta Putri all the way to Chengbee. Six thousand li. Just so we can talk."

Yongcheow sighed. "It—someone is working on it. It is only a start."

The path eased and sloped gently downhill as they approached Waiyi. As the day proceeded, Akeha said, "The Machinist movement is admirable. I agree: non-Tensors should have access to technology that doesn't rely on slackcraft. And there may be factions in the Tensorate who also agree. But the Protectorate will never relinquish its source of power. Your movement is doomed to misfortune."

"Good thing I don't believe in the fortunes, then."

"You believe in the will of your Almighty. How is that different?"

"The Almighty decides our circumstances. He doesn't decide our actions. It's what He gave us free will for."

"So you chose rebellion."

"We chose to *act*. Rebellion was the *Protectorate's* choice. They could easily have accepted our existence. But they didn't."

Akeha let this thought circulate, picking apart the

reasons he felt uncomfortable whenever free will was brought up. Even though he knew the real answer.

At the next stop, he finally confessed, "It's hard for me to believe in free will."

They had set up in a shallow limestone cave, a slanted scar in the side of the mountain forming the eastern forest border. Yongcheow looked sideways at him. "Let me guess. Because of your sister?"

"No matter what we did, her visions happened anyway. Future events *can* be set in stone. Where is your free will in that?"

Yongcheow folded careful hands over his belly. "But in those cases, you *did* do something, didn't you? You went to find the new Head Abbot. Your mother's purging Machinists. Some things might be fixed, but everything around them can be changed. *That's* the part that counts."

"A test. That's the Obedient belief, isn't it? Everything is a test from the heavens."

A considered silence simmered. Then Yongcheow spoke. "The saying goes, 'The black tides of heaven direct the courses of human lives.' To which a wise teacher said, 'But as with all waters, one can swim against the tide.'"

His gaze was unshakeable as it fixed on Akeha. "I chose to swim. So can you."

Chapter Sixteen

THEY WERE LESS THAN twenty li from Waiyi when the Protectorate caught up to them.

It was the snuffling that alerted Akeha. It came from the right, through a thicket of grass and shrubs, in the same tenor as a boar hunting for food. But there was no corresponding rustle, no crunch of massive porcine body through underbrush. Akeha squeezed Yongcheow's arm to stop him walking.

Yongcheow frowned. Akeha put a finger to his lips and directed the man to the cover of a peony bush.

The snuffling intensified. Something stirred within the blades and leaves.

The feathered head of a raptor snapped up from the vegetation.

Akeha forced his breathing to stay even. The creature's sleek head swiveled. It blinked.

He knew that ash coloring, the lichens of dark blue spread over the top of the head. A lifetime ago, there had been hatchlings in the Grand Monastery. In the mornings Akeha and Mokoya would throw wet slivers of meat to the waiting scramble of teeth.

It was said raptors had memories as long as their claws were sharp. "Tempeh," he whispered. "It's me. Akeha."

The raptor's nostrils flared.

A scout. The Protectorate had sent pugilists after Yongcheow. A betrayal on Thennjay's part? Hard to tell. He had no way of knowing Akeha was involved.

Tempeh pushed through the vegetation. An electric collar, hard and silver, sat in a wide band across its throat. Akeha frowned. The Grand Monastery's raptors didn't need to be controlled with shock collars—

Unless—

A targeted jolt through water-nature broke the clasp. As the collar clattered to the ground, it revealed a ribbon of scarred flesh, down and feathers burned off.

The raptor hissed, circling, surprised.

"It's over," Akeha said softly. "You don't have to—"

That thought was shattered by the high, rotating sound of a lightcraft. *Too late.* Akeha's senses sharpened in the Slack. A fully trained pugilist would have the advantage over him. Speed was his only chance. A knife to the throat before they could act—

The lightcraft crested over the brush, bearing a familiar figure. Master Yeo, the old disciplinarian from the monastery, clad in the sharp lines of Protectorate knit.

"Akeha." Her smile was a razor.

Half a second's delay. That's all it took. His knife sailed, but it was too late. Master Yeo didn't blink. Her cudgel moved: one end struck the knife into vegetation. The other end swung around, and an electrical bolt pierced Akeha.

He folded like a fan, veins on fire. But soon as he touched ground, he was struggling back up, fighting for clarity, sending a clumsy shockwave in her direction—

She whipped water-nature around his neck. Akeha gasped as it cut off blood and air. She would crush his vertebrae if she could. He pushed back in water-nature, tried to knock her down with another shockwave, but she resisted easily.

Spasming black bloomed in his vision. He fell to his knees, fighting for consciousness. She was too fast, too strong, too experienced. As his limbs collapsed under him, he sent a last, desperate tendril to Tempeh, trying to spur the raptor into action. Trying to override its fear and confusion.

Nothing. The black closed over him. Instinct drove his fingers to clutch uselessly at his throat. As he sank, all he saw was bright colors, flashes from childhood.

A loud, sharp crack filled the air.

The pressure released in an instant. Air flooded his lungs. A heartbeat's delay juddered by before he returned to his body, forcing it upright. His head sang with blood reasserting itself.

He felt Yongcheow before he saw the man. Warm hands grasped his arms as his eyes fought to focus. "Akeha? Are you all right? Please, say something."

He smelled the sulfur on him and understood.

Yongcheow's fingers pressed into his face. "Akeha."

He found words: "Where is she?"

Yongcheow glanced over his shoulder. Akeha struggled to numb feet, leaning on the other man, who winced. Akeha brushed a reassuring hand over the man's still-healing wound before staggering forward.

Master Yeo lay where she had fallen, but she was still alive. Blood patterned her face, fresh runnels crawling from her nose and mouth. The gunshot had punctured her chest, where an ocean of red was spreading. Her eyes turned toward Akeha as he crouched.

"Who sent you?" he asked. "Who did you come for?"

Her lips moved. Thick bubbles emerged, crimson mixed with frothy pink.

Tell me, he sent through the Slack. The twins' old trick sometimes worked with other people. But he felt nothing except her rage and confusion. And pain.

Akeha sighed and shut his eyes. He reached for water-nature, broad and shining, and snapped her spine cleanly across the base of her neck.

He stood up. "Protectorate uniform and rank. She defected from the monastery."

Yongcheow was trembling beside him.

"Are you all right?"

Yongcheow said nothing, head moving, jaw working, staring at the body on the ground.

Akeha gripped his arm. "Yongcheow."

"It happened so fast," he whispered. "I had no time to think." He had the bright, trembling eyes of someone witnessing death for the first time.

"You did what was necessary," Akeha said.

Yongcheow didn't respond. Akeha looked back down. A dead body at their feet. One in a long trail that had no beginning and probably no end. "Mother wouldn't have just sent regular troops to cut down Tensors in the purge. She'd send pugilists, like her. This woman had blood on her hands. I guarantee it."

Finally, slowly, Yongcheow nodded.

The raptor slunk in. Its narrow snout quested over the body, curious nostrils flaring, lips peeling back at the smell of fresh meat. Akeha hissed sharply and it backed away, rustling its feathers in submission. It still remembered the monastery. Still remembered him.

"There are no righteous deaths," Yongcheow whispered. "Only ones that cannot be avoided."

Akeha recognized the edict he was quoting from. He

had learned it, too, early in his career. It brought less and less comfort as the years went by.

"We need to bury her," Akeha said. "We can do that, at least."

Chapter Seventeen

"**HOW DO I KNOW** I can trust you?"

Lady Han's remaining eye, the one not curtained behind an embroidered patch, speared Akeha like an insect. The leader of the Machinists wore an eastern suit of jacket and pants, its sun-red fabric the brightest splash in a cavern cut out of raw granite. Between them, Yongcheow's scrolls lay isolated on a silver tray.

"I came of my own will," Akeha said.

"But for what purpose? The Protector's son, showing up at this precise point in time ... it's a bit convenient, isn't it?"

She'd had her subordinates seize him when they arrived at the hideout, almost spent from the long, steep journey from Waiyi to the caves. Yongcheow, sweat-glazed, had to stammer that he was a comrade, not a prisoner.

The other man was a reassuring weight in the periphery. "Perhaps it is the will of the Almighty," Akeha said.

"I have less tolerance for jokes than you think." She leaned on the table separating them.

Akeha had some memories of Lady Han, a cloud of impressions blurred by the stretch of intervening years. She had been close to Mother once, a beloved concubine, perhaps more. Akeha had been a child then; by the time he returned to the Great High Palace years later, she was gone. The missing eye was new.

He lifted his hands, blank palms out. "It was not a joke. I have no other explanation for you."

Her eye narrowed suspiciously.

"I have fled the consequences of my mother's rule for ten years. I was happy to live that way, in ignorance, as long as it didn't affect me. But this week, something changed." He shot a quick look at Yongcheow. "What else would you call it? Coincidence? It feels like more than that."

"The accidental rebel? The heaven-sent rebel? Neither sounds plausible to me."

He shrugged. What else could he offer?

Her guards shifted around them. Surrounded. He knew that he would walk away from this meeting a member of the movement, or not at all.

"All right," said Lady Han. "Prove it." She swept from the table, paced a small circle, and turned back to Akeha. "I have a task for you."

"Name it."

"Return to the Protectorate and kill the prophet."

It took two heartbeats to confirm he hadn't misheard. His skin cooled. "What?"

"She's your sister, isn't she? You can get close enough. Surprise her. She won't expect it."

Akeha's tongue stumbled over syllables. "She has nothing to do with—"

"She's a prophet," Lady Han said. "She sees things no one should know." A damning finger pointed to the scroll. "One prophecy, and over two hundred people dead or vanished. It has to stop."

"She has no control over what she sees," Akeha hissed.

"Exactly. The only way to stop her is to kill her. It sounds harsh, but it's true. Kill her, and your mother gets no more insights into our plans."

Akeha's chest crumpled like parchment fed to a flame. "You would see her killed for this?"

Yongcheow could not hold his tongue. "She's done nothing! If we're going to murder innocents, how are we any better than the Protectorate?"

Lady Han's head snapped in his direction. "Silence. We don't kill *lightly*." She turned back to Akeha. "One life could save countless others."

"You don't know that," Yongcheow said. "This is indefensible."

"If you want an assassin, find someone else," Akeha said through clenched teeth. "If this is the price for joining your movement, I choose death."

She stalked toward him. Akeha snapped into fighting mode, crisp in the Slack, even as his thoughts jumped in electric lines: Mokoya must be warned. He might die, but Yongcheow had the gun. He could strike, inflict maximum damage, give Yongcheow the chance to—

Lady Han stood before him. A diminutive woman with the force of a thunderstorm. His mind capsized, thoughts of resistance and murder scattering like spilled beans. She surveyed the riot of emotion snared upon his face. A smile blossomed across hers.

"A man of morals," she said. "Not what I expected of a smuggler."

He let her words and meaning sink through him. "You asked me to murder my own sister," he said, enunciating every syllable sharply.

"You come from a bloodline stained with remorseless familicides. I had to make sure of what you are."

A muscle seized in his jaw. He had little patience for those who used his sister's life as a plaything, a bargaining chip. He said, "If you wanted my loyalty, there were better ways of earning it."

She laughed and thumbed his chin, as though she considered herself a kindly aunt. "Don't think I'll go easy on you," she said, the corners of her eyes crinkling. "I will watch you very carefully, Sanao Akeha."

He breathed out as his heart rate rappelled down to normal. But his hands remained clenched in knuckled determination. "And I will do the same."

~

Their safe house in Waiyi was a gap-toothed cottage, cushioned by dirt rows once home to broad beans and pumpkins, now a forest of weeds. The sun had fallen. Yongcheow's gait remained stiff as they walked the stony, serpentine path toward its silhouette. One of Lady Han's guards had been a doctor, and his wounds had been made whole, but the pain lingered, as pain usually did.

"I've never met her," he admitted. "Lady Han. I'd heard her described as *remarkable,* but . . ."

"There must have been a reason Mother liked her," Akeha said. The fist of emotions in his chest had yet to ease open. The swift calculation he'd seen in Lady Han had left quite an impression. "And it would take more than courage to stand against the Protector."

"What do you think she would have done if you'd agreed?"

"I don't know." Unlikely that she would have grieved Mokoya's death.

Beside them, Tempeh snuffled in the tangled grass. The raptor had determinedly followed them into Waiyi, and Akeha had given up on chasing it away. Freed from the painful confines of Protectorate control, the creature had decided what it wanted.

"What you said to Lady Han. About the will of the Almighty. Did you mean that?"

The warm, damp evening air was a blessing. "It felt like the right thing to say."

Yongcheow hesitated. "I don't know how else to put it, but . . . look. To be Obedient is to live with constant ridicule. People call you superstitious, uneducated, backward. Behind your back and to your face. I don't care what you believe, but don't say those things just to make fun of them."

"I wasn't." Akeha looked at his feet. "The past few days . . . I don't know how to explain them. I—" He sucked in another gift of air. "I have a lot to think about."

Tempeh ran ahead of them toward the house. Five yields away, it stopped, head alert, feathers erect along its spine. Akeha stopped Yongcheow.

"What is it?" he whispered.

Akeha gestured for silence. Within the house the Slack hung in a way that sent a frisson through him. A familiar presence waited.

Tempeh stood by the door and rumbled.

His heart a burr in his chest, Akeha pushed the door open.

At the dining table a figure, robe-clad, stood and pulled its gray hood back. Her eyes fixed on his, shining. "Keha."

Mokoya.

She looked exactly the same. She looked entirely different. The years had changed her face, but she was still his sister, his twin. The same cheekbones, the same hooded eyes, the same crooked mouth. She had not painted her face. She was still dressed as a nun. And her hair clung to her scalp like a penitent's or mourner's.

"So it's true," she said. "You've joined the Machinists."

He stepped into the house, Yongcheow behind him. The door clicked shut. His lips, out of practice, struggled to form her name. What came out instead was "What are you doing here?"

She stepped toward him, hands held up to touch his face. "Keha."

His chest was full; his heart was empty. "How did you find me?"

"I saw you."

He broke away from her, turning so she couldn't see the expression on his face. "You dreamed this?"

"A week ago."

A week ago. A black snake of fear coiled. He looked at her and saw that under her cloak, she still wore the box that collected her visions, her dreams. Everything she prophesied, the Tensorate collected and studied. *A week ago.* A torrent of words broke through: "What else did you see? What else do they know?"

"Who?" She followed his line of sight. "Keha—no. No! I destroyed that vision. You *can* do that, you know. I don't hand *everything* over to Mother. If she'd hurt you, I—" She couldn't complete the thought.

Akeha tightened his lips. Mokoya gave the impression she was made of glass, bright and clear and brilliant, and one blow away from shattering. She did not need to know about the grave they'd left in the forest.

"Your friends are safe," she said. "I wouldn't betray them to Mother."

The snake within him struck. "But you let her have the one with the attack on the palace. The one that started the purges."

He saw the shudder that went through her. "I had to! I *had* to. They were carrying *explosives,* Keha. Hundreds would have died, many of them innocents, if I'd done nothing. How could I have predicted what she would do with it?"

"She's *Mother.* What did you think she would do with it? Pardon everyone involved? Say oh, it's nothing, there's nothing to worry about?"

"Keha, I—"

"No, she's right." Yongcheow's interruption was fueled

by a core of panic. "Unwarranted as it is, your mother's retaliation would have been worse if they'd succeeded. If they'd blown up a whole section of the Great High Palace, she'd have had people executed in the street."

Mokoya swallowed audibly. Memories crashed to the surface: his sister as a child, shaking and weeping in dark beds after a vision ripped through her. She'd done nothing to deserve this.

Twelve years apart, and the first thing he did was upset her. Where were the tender words he had imagined would burst forth when they saw each other again, older and wiser and settled in their places in the world? "Moko." He brushed his palm against her cheek. She flinched, and something in him broke, but then she leaned into his touch. He waited until he could speak without shaking. "Why are you here?"

She took his hand, grasped it between hers. "I want you to come home."

He shook his head. "Moko, I—"

"I'm pregnant."

He stopped, stunned. "What?"

A smile crept across the pale trench of her face. "The child won't be along for months, but—Thennjay and I have been trying for a while, and finally—"

"Congratulations," he said, softly, in wonder.

"Come back," she said, pressing into his hand.

"Come back to the monastery. Thennjay can give you asylum. You'll be safe. Mother can't do anything. Please, Keha." Her voice cracked, equal parts hope and sorrow. "Come home. I don't want to raise a child who's never met you."

Akeha's hand shook in hers. He imagined her child listening to their mother's stories, trying to conjure up an uncle they knew only through words. His resolve softened, began to melt. It was tempting, so tempting, to say yes, to be forgiven, to return, to shape a glorious, shining future—

He turned away, terrified. There was Yongcheow, in a corner, struggling to keep his expression neutral. No matter what Akeha chose, he would still be here. He couldn't return to the capital. And the spider-grasp of the Protectorate would continue to ensnare Machinists, out here and everywhere. That would still happen.

No. He turned to her. "I can't." Her mouth moved to register protests, and he said, "Moko, listen. You can't stay here. It's not safe. You have to go back."

"Keha—"

"Go back home, Moko. You have a new family coming. Focus on your future. Forget about me."

"Forget?"

He held her face in his hands. "What you and Thennjay are doing in the monastery—that's important. Someone has to fight Mother from within. But that was never going to be me."

Because he had always known, even as a child, that he was the lightning, while she was the fire in the core of planets. And the world needed both. Revolutions needed both. Someone had to wield the knives, but someone also had to write the treaties.

"My place is out here. You understand, don't you?"

She trembled, as angry as she was devastated. "I've missed you so much."

"I know." And, great Slack, did he know. Deep in the pit of his belly, reaching up to suffocate him on the longest nights. He crushed her in a hug. "I know, Moko. I've missed you too."

He let her cry herself empty on his shoulder. And later, when she had gone, as he crumpled against a solid surface struggling for sense and air, he let Yongcheow hold him, until he, too, was empty.

Much later, in the dark where they lay together in bed, skin to skin, Yongcheow asked, "Why didn't you go with her?"

Akeha found Yongcheow's hand and curled fingers against fingers. "Let the black tides of heaven direct our lives," he murmured. He turned to look at his partner. "I choose to swim."

PART FOUR

MOTHER

Chapter Eighteen

YEAR THIRTY-FIVE

WHEN THE SMOKE CLEARED, it left nothingness in its wake.

It wasn't nothingness, exactly—there was debris and churned mud and a thick overcoat of sticky char. Lumps of organic ballast swelled from the ground, leaving the burnt landscape undulating like a graveyard. But as Akeha walked through the spongy ruin of the test site, he felt only nothingness around him. Nothingness clawed at his back and sides where the living trunks of linden trees had stood. Nothingness yawned in the cauterized air where there should have been the tang of nectar and sap and well-fed humus. Nothingness blanketed the muffled soil under his feet where once lay a thick layer of crisp autumn shedding.

The blast radius around him was a hundred yields wide. Akeha had stood on a nearby hill and shot the test device into the middle of the woods, a scallop of temperate wilderness just outside the port city of Bun-shim. He'd made the weapon right, he thought, following the directives scribbled in the defector's spindly hand. He'd performed the slackcraft as instructed, melting the gas within the tiny steel shell with so much fire- and earth-nature that it was no longer gas but something they had no name for. He'd held on to that seething, violent miasma for as long as his focus had allowed, letting go at the last possible moment, freeing the terrible energy that had accumulated within. The resulting shockwave—a balloon of gray shrouding bloodred—had knocked him off his feet from hundreds of yields away.

So this is what it does, he thought, walking through the carbonized aperture left behind. He'd known the device was a weapon, but he'd expected something like a big firecracker or a thunder bomb. Not this. The edges of the explosive wound harbored recognizable fragments—half-melted trees and charred mounds that had once been animals, felled not knowing what had hit them. But here, in the middle of the crater, the heat and light had been so intense that nothing was left except fine black ash. Everything had been pulverized at the moment of detonation.

The air felt *wrong.* Something lingered in it, worming through the Slack in glowing, infinitesimal paths. Coming down the hill toward the crater Akeha had put a barrier around himself, a protective layer of forest-nature just in case the blast had been toxic. That barrier was now under attack, being slowly clawed through by the changed air. As though the atoms of the dead things, too, had turned into ghosts that wanted to possess him. Wanted to drag him into dissolution with them.

The defector had come from one of the Tensorate's secret divisions: sixteen Tensors playing on the radiant fringe of slackcrafting knowledge, manipulating the fine forces at the boundary of the five natures. One mad day the defector had killed her fifteen colleagues, burned the lab to the ground, and fled the capital city with the last copies of their manuscript. Standing in the middle of the blast grounds, feeling like death incarnate, a destroyer of worlds, Akeha began to understand why.

This weapon needed a name. Akeha had another prototype swinging from his belt like a moon, and it begged for taxonomy that bayed of what it could do. He thought about fire and death and otherworldly annihilation. The word "jinn" drifted toward him. "Ifrit." Perhaps.

Some time later Yongcheow found him kneeling before what remained of a deer, reciting a guilt-tinged prayer for its soul.

"So it works," he said hesitantly, looking out over the ruined landscape. "You did it."

Akeha unfolded himself. "Yes."

"Congratulations?" The sentence came out half statement, half question; Yongcheow didn't know what to make of the destruction either. He'd put up his own barrier, following Akeha's example. Yongcheow scanned the lines of his lover's face until confidence returned to him, then gently stroked his cheek. "I knew you could do it. I'm sure Lady Han will be delighted."

Akeha, standing at the gates of Hell, said, "That's what I'm afraid of."

Yongcheow didn't sigh, but the look on his face was grim. Akeha changed the topic. "I take it the exchange went well?"

"Yes. I've sent the merchant on his way." Old habits made them speak in vague terms, even with nothing left alive to eavesdrop on them.

"Good." He looked at the cloth parcel in Yongcheow's other hand and frowned. "You brought dinner."

A smile beamed through the gloom on Yongcheow's face. "I cooked. It turned out surprisingly well. This time."

The strangeness in the air chewed at him still. Akeha suppressed a shudder. "You shouldn't have brought it here. Now it's contaminated." By what, he didn't know. But just to be safe: "We'll have to get rid of it."

Yongcheow studied his expression and came to a grave understanding. He chuckled purposefully. "If you didn't want to eat my cooking, you could have just said so."

He emptied the containers over the poisoned ground. Soup noodles, the broth thick with nuts and spices, a recipe from his mother's side of the family. Guilt flared through Akeha: it smelled good, especially by Yongcheow's standards. He'd have to ask him to try again later. To make up for it.

~

They had vinegar noodles from a roadside stall back in Bunshim, perched on a bench next to the lively gullet of the city's legendary perfumed quarter. Immersed in the warm glow of sunballs, the tart vapor of noodle broth, and the jabber of the drunk and the soon-to-be drunk, Akeha finally felt the unease quietly drain out of him, leaving him a normal person again.

The defector had killed herself not long after she'd passed her manuscripts to the Machinists. A washerwoman had gone up to her room in the safe house and found her curled into a stiff comma, a vial of poison spilled on the floor. Akeha had struggled to understand this—why flee, why spend agonizing weeks evading capture, if death had always been the final destination? If suicide had been the plan, why not perish in the flames with the rest of her division?

Now he understood. She had wanted the Machinists

to know. Just in case she hadn't been thorough enough. This was her insurance, her gamble against his mother's ruthlessness. Her hope that both sides, understanding the horror of what had been wrought, would never resort to using these—what had he decided to call them again? These weapons.

"They're too risky to be effective," he said, partly to Yongcheow, partly to himself. "The slackcraft is too complex; most Tensors won't have that much focus. If you do it wrong, you'll destroy your own troops."

"No doubt." Yongcheow was thoughtful. "But *you* can do it."

"I can. I'm not like most Tensors."

"Isn't it a good thing you're on our side, then."

They watched a dancer with a green ribbon in her hair flirting with a ship's captain. "I nearly forgot," Yongcheow said, in a tone meaning he hadn't forgotten at all. "The merchant had something for you. A small surprise from the Grand Monastery."

A flutter in his chest. "A letter?"

"Better than that." Yongcheow reached into his sleeves and withdrew a cloth bundle the size of a plum. The same size as the yet-unnamed weapons. "It's a gift. From your niece."

"My niece." Mokoya's daughter. He unwrapped the bundle delicately.

Thick burlap peeled away to reveal a corkscrew of gleaming white petals, crudely shaped but recognizable as a lotus blossom. The grain of the ceramic whispered of shaping and firing by slackcraft. Akeha turned it around with vigilant fingertips, marveling at its construction.

Under the glass piece lay a note on lovingly crumpled gray paper. Unsteady brushstrokes read: *To Uncle Akeha, from Eien.*

Yongcheow watched him struggle to contain his expression and snorted. Akeha didn't care, caught in the swell of warmth like a tidal wave. "Her slackcraft is improving," he said.

"Well, with a mother like that, and her father the Head Abbot, I would be surprised if it didn't."

The glass lotus lay dwarfed by the palm of his hand, and he was seized by a sudden terror of dropping it. He had to find a safe place for it, somewhere padded and concealed. *To Uncle Akeha, from Eien.* With all the horrors in the world, it was easy to forget there were wonders too.

"Thank you," he said to Yongcheow, even though his words were directed a thousand li away, at a smiling child he had never met and who had never met him.

~

They were threading toward sleep when Yongcheow ambushed him. "Have you ever thought about having children?"

Akeha froze. "What?" Remarkable that after the day's happenings, the question still managed to unsettle him. His heart spun in his chest as he scrambled for an answer, a drowning man seeking dry land. "I don't know. Why? Are you thinking about having children?"

"I asked you first."

I'm the least fatherly person I know. "What would we do with a child on the run?"

"Mmh."

Silence settled over the room. Akeha pushed up on one elbow, trying to read his partner's face in the gloom. The clouded moonlight gave him nothing. The unspoken agreement was that neither of them was interested in parenthood. Or so he'd thought. "Yongcheow. *Do* you want children?"

"No. I was just curious. Just wondering."

With Yongcheow there was no such thing as *just wondering.* "What's wrong?" When the man didn't answer, he pressed further: "What were you really asking?"

Yongcheow let the appropriate beats go by before firing the shot. "Why won't you go back to Chengbee?"

Akeha sank onto the bed with a sigh. It always came down to this. Every year, every turning of the seasons,

Yongcheow would ask him the same question, and he would give up the same excuses, the same nonanswers. When would he tire of this back-and-forth?

His lover said, "It's been years. The girl's growing up fast."

"I know."

"Why won't you go back? Even for a visit?"

"I can't." Akeha wasn't sure he could explain it in words to himself, much less someone else. Why couldn't he return to the place of his birth? Because tigers prowled in the woods, and giant snakeheads circled in the water. He just couldn't. "Now's not the time."

Yongcheow stayed silent for a few seconds, and Akeha knew the pensive expression on his face without looking. "I want to see her too."

"I know. Someday you will. When the time is right." An indefinite hope of things changing, a watery promise. Akeha listened to the cycle of Yongcheow's breathing, dreading further interrogation. But none was forthcoming. Apparently satisfied with Akeha's dilute answers, Yongcheow drifted off into sleep.

~

"I know what to call them."

"What? What time is it?"

"I said, I know what to call the weapons."

"Akeha, go back to sleep."

"Sunballs. We should call them sunballs."

" . . . what?"

"They explode with the brightness of the sun. We should call them sunballs."

"You . . . I can't believe you woke me for this."

"I thought you would find it funny."

"I'll find it funny when it's not the unmentionable crack of night. Go back to sleep, you turtle bastard."

"I love you."

Chapter Nineteen

THINGS STARTED TO GO WRONG after prayers at first sunrise. Pain seared through Akeha's veins; he doubled over as though he had been shot, breath emerging in ragged gasps.

"What is it?" Yongcheow asked, alarm suffusing him as every possibility from poison to a hidden arrow to a heart attack flashed through his imagination. "Akeha!"

Akeha couldn't answer. He staggered across the room, grasping for his pack, searching for something that burned in his mind like a coal brand. A sense of danger had hit him, an impression of suffering so powerful the blood struggled to reach his head. He felt like he was dying. Perhaps he was.

His hands found what he was looking for. A flat, black medallion of volcanic rock, its center scooped out and replaced with faceted glass. It was one half of a pair, entangled in the Slack like talkers. Thennjay had the other half. When the glass changed colors, it meant something had happened. It meant *Return to the city. Something is wrong.* An emergency that couldn't wait for a letter to wend its way to them.

Akeha had carried it for years, and for years it had remained dark. Until now. In his shaking hand, the glass
glowed red, the color of blood fresh from the vein.

"What is it?" Yongcheow asked. "What does it mean?"

The initial blast of pain had broken over him, leaving
numb chill in its receding wake. Akeha closed white fingers around the stone. "Mokoya."

~

Because they had no safe house in Bunshim, they stayed
at an inn of unsavory reputation, an all-hours place where
patrons could be trusted to turn a blind eye to anything.
A mix of weathered scowls and wild-eyed hunger
prowled its wooden interiors, selling everything from sex
to drugs to murder. Akeha, having gathered his belongings, went downstairs to find someone willing to lend
him a carriage.

He could not get Thennjay on the talker. Whatever
had happened in the capital, it was serious. Not knowing
was the worst part, the part that was eating a hole in his
stomach, the part that was sending his thoughts on bright
and terrifying excursions. Had Mother done something?
Was Mokoya hurt? Was she dead?

He thought of the sunball he carried, and of the

insatiable flames that had consumed the defector's lab in Chengbee. What if—?

All-hours establishments followed neither sun and moon nor day and night. The ground floor was unpleasantly drunk in the collar of time after first sunrise, shouts shaking the rafters and fumes of spilled wine stinging the eyes. Akeha, having put on a reasonable mask of calm, stood three steps up from the chaos and surveyed the scattershot tables for faces he recognized.

Behind him Yongcheow said, "That's Banyar the silk merchant, isn't it?"

Banyar owed them a favor from years back. She was tucked in a corner, plying a boy far too young for her with drink. She liked to travel in ostentatious conveyances, lacquered with gold, topped with riotous carvings, laden with more silk than a concubine's quarters. Not the best way to slip into the capital unnoticed.

"We can ask her," Akeha said.

As he descended, a table of revelers tore into his focus. A group of rough men, faces shiny and red and unfamiliar, squalling dialect from the lower quarters of Chengbee. The stink of money lingered around them. Akeha recognized the wretched pattern of tourists on a binge, here to taste Bunshim's seedy delights, spending ill-gotten wealth on the golden dancers and pleasure ships in the harbor.

As he walked by their table, his anxiety expanded till it clotted his heart. Laughter peppered their conversation, which stewed in a foul delight. Some tragedy had just happened in the capital, some sort of explosion. Their oblique references were hard to parse, a story with no head and no tail. But someone had died. Someone important.

His chest twisted. Mokoya, her body dissolving in a sunball flare.

A man with a thin, wormy mustache commanded the largest share of the attention. He said, "If she was so damn powerful, how come she didn't predict this disaster?"

The table shook under open-palmed howling. Akeha turned to him and said, "Tell me what happened."

His companions crackled with more laughter as he said, "Oh, you haven't heard the latest out of Chengbee?"

Slowly, through the roaring in his ears, Akeha repeated, "Tell me what happened."

One of the man's more observant friends tugged at his sleeve, whispered in his ear. The man squinted, suddenly hugely interested in Akeha's face. Then his laughing returned threefold. "Oh, you're her brother, are you? Oh, pity, pity!"

He stood up, drunk beyond all sense. "Do you see this, friends? This man, the Protector's son, standing here, and he has no inkling! No inkling of what's happened to his sister!" He slapped Akeha on the arm, pulled at his shoulder.

"Is she dead?" was all he could manage.

"Oh, not so, not so! But she will be soon, I hear! Too bad about that half-breed brat of hers, eh? Incinerated, I hear."

His high, thin voice pierced like a bee sting. Mokoya's daughter. His niece. "Incinerated."

"Yes. Monastery went up like a firework!" As Akeha felt the skin across his knuckles tighten, the man continued crowing, "Must be a relief for your mother, huh?" His mouth was wide, full of ugly yellow teeth. "No more embarrassment from a Gauri half-breed running—"

By the time Akeha registered what he was doing, his hand was fisted in the man's hair and a knife was halfway to his throat. It sliced clean, under the jaw, spraying him with fine, warm blood.

Akeha dropped the body first, then the knife.

The dead man's companions shot to their feet, and he knew then that these were people who hurt other people for a living.

Air ignited over his clenched right fist. He would burn them, peel blackened skin from bubbling flesh—

"Akeha!"

Yongcheow. Akeha did not budge. He was facing five

men. They would be no problem. He could see the same knowledge on their faces, as they realized who and what it was they faced. What they had unleashed.

Around him, the inn emptied in a determined, quiet fashion. The patrons had seen things like this happen before, and they didn't like how it ended.

"Oi, oi." Tze-Fong, the inn's owner, moved her bulk between the abandoned tables, indignant hands on solid hips. "You going to pay for my furniture?"

Akeha did not back down. But neither did he attack.

Tze-Fong glared at the five men. "Get out," she snapped. When they looked at each other, she said, "Did you hear me? You want him to kill you? Get out!"

They scrambled.

Only when the last of them had crossed the inn's threshold did Akeha extinguish the flame he'd created. "Tsk," Tze-Fong clucked, looking at the body on the floor, soaking in its own blood.

"I'm sorry for the mess," Akeha said. His ears rang and rang and rang, a chorus of bells that had no end.

Tze-Fong's face twisted. "Don't need. This one, he burned one of my girls yesterday. Threw hot soup in her face. Bastard." She kicked one splayed arm. "I'll clean up."

"Akeha." Yongcheow's warm, familiar hand descended on his shoulder. "Are you all right?"

He shook his head.

Tze-Fong sighed. "It's true, you know. What the bas-tard said."

Akeha looked at her. "My sister?"

She nodded. "I talked to somebody in the capital ear-lier. There was a big explosion, some accident or some-thing. The little girl died." She looked at Akeha's face. "Sorry."

"What kind of explosion, how big?"

Tze-Fong shrugged helplessly. Of course she wouldn't know—how would she know?

"What about my sister? Did they say anything about my sister?"

"That one—don't know, sorry. It's all rumors only. No official announcement. Maybe won't have one at all."

He breathed deeply. "I need a carriage to the city."

"I don't have carts free. But I have one horse carriage. You want? It's only a bit slower."

Akeha nodded. Words had died in his mouth.

Chapter Twenty

HER NAME WAS EIEN, and she was six. At the age of three, she had told her mother she was a girl, and had not changed her mind thereafter. A light capture of her, sent by Thennjay with one of his dutiful, seasonal letters, showed a nut-brown child with bright eyes round as marbles, and fishbowl-shaped hair. The light capture came on a new kind of scroll, which looped through five seconds of the girl breaking into a gap-toothed giggle, something reminiscent of her mother in the way she ducked her head.

She liked animals and the color yellow. Outside of that, Akeha knew nothing. What her laugh sounded like. Whether she skipped while running down corridors. Or if she liked running down corridors at all.

Akeha managed to get Thennjay on the talker as they left the city. The man's voice, iron-weight, tonelessly told Akeha what he already knew: There had been an explosion in the monastery. Eien was dead. Mokoya was grievously hurt.

An attack? Akeha had asked, fearing poisoned air and contaminated water.

No, Thennjay said, *an accident. One of our own.*

Something built by the Machinists had gone wrong. Not a blow dealt by the Protectorate. Not a gaping mouthful of demonic fire. Not yet.

Come quickly, Thennjay said. A carnivorous fear had hollowed out his voice. *I don't know how long she has left.*

The horse carriage rattled over stones in the road. Bunshim was just a day's travel away from the capital, but to Akeha, slowly and coolly detaching from the surface of the world, the journey was interminable. It felt like the sun rose and fell sixty times while he was trapped in that wooden box, his niece's gift held loosely in his fingers. He couldn't think of it as her *last gift.* Those words refused to settle in his mind.

He stared desolately at the smooth lobes and flutes of porcelain. There were scars on his palms: small ones, not-so-small ones. He tried to connect memory to each one. Nothing.

Yongcheow, leaning across the carriage, touched his face. "Akeha."

A shudder lanced through him, pulling him back into the present. "I'm sorry."

"There's no need to apologize."

"I shouldn't have killed that man."

Yongcheow sighed. "Probably not." He brushed aside the curtain of Akeha's fringe. "It's been a while since . . ."

Akeha shut his eyes. He'd never told Yongcheow this, but he kept a tally of every person whose blood he had spilled. He tried to remember their faces and their circumstances, even if he never learned their names. It was like a mantra for him, whispered in his head on long nights when he couldn't sleep, when he tried to remember the kind of person he was. The kind of person he had been. It started with the man with the knife in the alley, not long after he had fled the capital. And then the two boys after that, not much older than he was, just as hungry, just as desperate. On and on.

Yesterday, that tally had stood at sixty-two. Now it was sixty-three.

"Listen," Akeha said. "You have to stay out of the city. We'll go all the way to the border, and drop you off at the cottage there."

"Akeha—"

"No. It's too dangerous. For all we know, this could be a trap set by my mother. I can face her—I *will* face her—but I want you to stay away." Yongcheow frowned; Akeha clamped an iron hand over his. "Please. Your research work is important. The Machinists can't lose us both at once."

"*I* can't lose you at all," Yongcheow whispered.

He looked away. "I'm sorry."

The finite nature of the world meant that the horse

carriage eventually did draw up to the boundary of the capital city. Akeha gave the carriage master a gold tal for his troubles and sent him on his way.

"You'll stay hidden, won't you?" he asked Yongcheow.

"I'll stay hidden *behind* you, if you don't let me walk by your side."

"Yongcheow, listen—"

"No, *you* listen. You keep cutting me out of your family's business, and I've had enough. Whatever lies in the capital scares you. I know. I understand. But it's important to you. That makes it important to me too. I don't want to be left out of it."

"Do you understand the danger I'll put you in?"

"Do I look like an idiot?" His hands met Akeha's and latched on with a magnetic grip. "I'll follow you anywhere, Akeha. You just have to let me."

Yongcheow's words were backed by the strength of mountains, by the conviction that would lead an unarmed man to stand firm against three soldiers twice his size. Akeha looked at him, really looked, and saw someone whose loss would tear a good fatal chunk out of him.

Akeha shut his eyes and offered a prayer to the Almighty.

He said, "You'll have to stay hidden behind me. We can't be seen together. It's too risky. Do you understand?"

Yongcheow didn't, not at first. But then he did, and the realization that Akeha was relenting after all dawned across his face. He nodded, his fingers betraying only a brief tremble against Akeha's.

Chapter Twenty-one

THENNJAY MET THEM ON the steps of the monastery. "Akeha," he said.

That rolling thunder voice had not been changed by the seasons. It was deeper, perhaps. Roughened, chafed by the weight of the world around him. But it still bore the same magnetism, the same compelling gravity that enveloped the listener in its orbit. Or maybe Akeha was comparing the present to an unreliable past. He stood in front of a man who had, for the past eighteen years, existed as little more than a voice over the talker and generous, looping script on parchment. Thennjay was no longer the lithe boy he'd once met and barely remembered. The years had broadened his chest, added heft to his leonine features. His beard flowed as freely as his abbot's robes.

He stood waiting, tall and glorious even in his grief, and Akeha could not find it in himself to approach the man. He stopped several yields away, an ocean of missed opportunities and wasted futures roiling between them.

It was Thennjay who closed the gap, arms enveloping

Akeha in a great embrace, one wrapped around his back, one cradling his head. In that rush of warmth and scent, all the anxiety and fear that had built in him finally came unbound, bursting within his chest like overripe fruit. He gripped Thennjay hard around the spine, and whispered, "I am so sorry," over and over, eighteen years of penitence spilling from the broken dam of his lips.

Yongcheow bowed graciously when Akeha introduced him. "At last we meet," he told the Head Abbot. "I've heard nothing but wild stories about you." Thennjay extracted a smile from somewhere for Yongcheow's sake. They should have met under happier circumstances. This, too, was Akeha's fault.

He said: "Mokoya—is she . . ."

Thennjay looked stricken.

Akeha wet his lips. "I want to see her. Please."

"Come," he said.

~

They had put Mokoya in one of the stone halls of meditation. Breaking its age-old rules, Thennjay explained, the monastery had accepted a large number of adult initiates in recent years, and some of them had been high-ranking doctors in the Tensorate. Refugees, in so many words, but now their skills had saved Mokoya's life.

Not saved, exactly, Thennjay told him. They had tried their best, and she was still alive, but only just.

"Tell me what happened," Akeha said.

Eien loved animals. She especially adored the monastery's raptor pack. Every morning, at first sunrise, Mokoya would indulgently take her to feed them.

They'd done this too, when they were children.

Except that this was a time of insurrection, and the monastery was no longer a simple house of tranquility. The backyard was home to a congregation of Machinist devices in various stages of testing. Numbered among them was a gas-compression heater.

As they found out that morning, there were flaws in its design. Fatal ones.

"Eien was the closest to the explosion," Thennjay said. "Mokoya . . . she . . ." He gestured to the stone hall they were approaching, unable to complete his sentence.

A raised bed had been installed in the middle of the hall, a fragile thing dwarfed by the vastness around it. Two doctors stood in attendance.

Akeha's steps forward took eternity after eternity. The patient lay half smothered in white sheets. He couldn't focus on her face, couldn't focus on anything. There was so much wrong, so much to look at.

Mokoya was unclothed, swathed in a sarcophagus of bandages through which red seeped like ink. Her right arm was encased in a bubbling, irregular cocoon; a cocoon that looked like it was made of living flesh; a cocoon that hummed like a thousand wasps were at work within. Above it, transparent jelly clung to the right half of her face, a thick gel that masked nothing of the seething, burnt flesh beneath. A mask of ridged gristle smothered her nose and mouth, flapping wetly like fish gills.

Underneath all of that, it was still Mokoya. His sister. The person he had come into this world with—the person he could not imagine this world without—

"They're rebuilding her arm with a lizard graft," Thennjay said. "But her lungs are too badly burnt. There isn't enough healthy tissue left to rebuild them, and we can't use a graft."

"She's dying," he whispered. He wanted to touch her. He was afraid to.

Mokoya's eyes flicked open, wide and staring.

"Moko?" He felt her come alive in the Slack, tangled in the webbing of connections the doctors had woven around her. "Moko!"

Her eyes shot back and forth, then zeroed in on his face. Her reaction—recognition—preceded a panicked response, as she struggled to sit up, clawing at the living mask with her left hand. As Akeha reached for her, the doctors burst forward with overlapping calls of "Tensor Sanao—"

Mokoya pulled the mask off, gasping, barely making out the words "Keha—"

"No, no." He held her, supporting her head, her body, terrified of making things worse. "Moko, please—"

Her skin instantly slid toward grayness. Air rattled through the ruins of her throat and lungs as she clutched at Akeha's face with her remaining hand. Her blue lips moved, trying to form words. "You came." A misshapen smile ghosted across her face. "I wanted to see you—I—"

I'm so glad, his twin whispered in his mind. He felt relief flood her. She only wanted to see him one last time.

Another rattle. She slumped in his arms, eyes rolling backward, mouth falling open. Akeha, arms locking up, screamed her name. He couldn't let go, she had to wake up, she had to look at him, breathe—Mokoya—

Thennjay pulled him away and clung to him, nails digging into skin, as the doctors reattached the mask and coaxed breath back into her. "She's alive," Thennjay whispered, holding on, rocking slightly. "She's alive." He said it over and over like a prayer.

Thennjay released him only when the doctors stepped back, Mokoya's condition stabilized. Yongcheow squeezed his arm, fingers distorting the flesh. "How can I save her?" Akeha asked. His voice echoed through the hollows of his throat. He looked at Thennjay. Looked at the doctors. "How can I help?"

Thennjay said, "You're identical twins."

It took half a minute for Thennjay's meaning to register in the bedlam of his mind. Akeha filled his lungs, the withered aching things hanging exhausted in his chest. He glanced at Yongcheow for a brief, confirmatory moment. "Take whatever you need," he said. "Do it now. I want you to save her."

Into the silence that ensued came a cascade of sound: feet, running. A breathless acolyte tumbled into the hall, white with fear. "Venerable One," he gasped. "Protectorate troops—what do we do?"

The acolyte was little more than a child, his voice only beginning to change in his throat. "How many?" Thennjay asked.

"A hundred, more, I'm not sure. A lot. They have weapons."

"They're here for me," Akeha said.

Thennjay shot him a look, and Akeha knew he was going to confront Mother's troops alone, to pretend that he wasn't harboring a dangerous fugitive. "Stay here."

"Thenn—"

"Please. Stay with Mokoya. Watch her."

He watched Thennjay leave, broad-backed and determined. A sour tide of emotion crested and spent itself within him, nervous energy trickling down to his fingers, his calves, his feet. There were many ways this could end, none of them happy. Akeha had to do something, and only a narrow band of choices were left to him.

He looked at Yongcheow, as if to say, *This is what I was afraid of. This is why I could never return.*

Yongcheow's lips charted a grim line. He knew Akeha too well. He understood what was going to happen.

One of the doctors tending to Mokoya was significantly older than the other, her eyes lined with age, if not wisdom. Akeha looked at her. "You need lung tissue," he said. "How long will it take to extract it?"

The woman sighed. "It's a delicate procedure. First, the donor has to be sedated—"

"How *long*."

"Hours, at least."

Hours they did not have, not now. He stroked Mokoya's forehead, neatening the line of her hair over her cold skin.

He looked at the old doctor. "Can you harvest the tissue from a dead body?"

"*Akeha,*" Yongcheow whispered.

She blinked, visibly swallowing. "I—we—yes, but it has to be relatively soon after death."

"How soon?"

The doctor shook her head; she understood the thrust of Akeha's questioning. "Sir, I cannot—"

"Just tell me," Akeha said. He tried to be gentle.

She could not meet his eyes. "I would guess within three hours of death, if not sooner."

Half a sun-cycle. A narrow band, but not unreasonable. "Thank you," he said.

"You can't," Yongcheow said, preempting his argument entirely. "I won't let you."

He wanted to say, *You should have stayed away if you didn't want to see this.* Instead he cupped Yongcheow's chin. "We got this far. It's more than I could have asked for."

"If you die, your sister dies too. You know that. Your mother won't allow otherwise."

We were born together; we die together. "Mokoya would never let the movement be sacrificed for her sake. Neither will I."

A stubborn set of the lip. "I'll go with you."

"Mother will have you killed. Her only interest is in me. If you come along, she'll use you against me."

"I can't just let you go."

"You have to."

Yongcheow gripped his arms hard, as if he could prevent Akeha leaving through sheer physical force. "Yongcheow, I want you to stay here. Look after Thennjay. And Mokoya, if the Almighty permits." *If a miracle happens.* "Do this for me."

Yongcheow mouthed the syllables of his name, unable to put strength behind them. Akeha kissed him hard, their lips issuing a commandment of desire, playing a symphony of desperation.

When their bodies parted, it felt like a continent splitting. He gripped Yongcheow's hand, then put his hand over his heart. "His peace be with you," he said.

Then he leaned over Mokoya and pressed his lips to her forehead. He whispered words he should have said years ago, instead of leaving it until now, when there was a good chance she wasn't hearing them at all, her eyes dark and swollen shut. He had to go. He *had* to go. He pretended he wasn't shaking as he walked away.

~

Eyes trailed Akeha's pilgrimage to the front of the monastery: acolytes and senior pugilists and everyone in between, peering from windows and behind pillars. The ranks of the pious had been swelled with Thennjay's Machinist refugees, protected thus far by the ancient codes that granted the Grand Monastery autonomy over its affairs. If they weren't on a list before they fled here, they were safe from Mother's grasp.

Until now.

This was how the raids always started, soldiers banging

on doors suspected to conceal known Machinists. Next it would be a line of people squatting against the wall, heads down, hands tied behind their backs, soon to be sucked into the fetid underbelly of the Protectorate. Vanished. So great was the appetite of empire that it would not even spit out the bones.

He would not let that happen here.

Akeha came to the cushion of garden between the monastery and the path to the city. Thennjay was locked in verbal hostility with a woman dressed in a general's colors. Arrayed on the steps below them were hundreds of soldiers, guns in hand. One of them scratched an itchy calf, another shifted on restless feet. Their impatience pinged on the Slack, a constellation of microtwitches.

Akeha stepped forward. "Thennjay."

The man turned, an oceanic wash of fear and dismay overcoming him. "Leave them alone," Akeha said to the pinch-faced general. "I'll come with you. I want to speak to my mother."

Thennjay rumbled. "Akeha—"

"Don't." He looked over the columns of waiting Protectorate troops. "Don't get innocents killed protecting me."

He had been running from this for long enough. It was time to put it to an end.

Akeha pulled Thennjay close and kissed him, for old times' sake. Thennjay whispered his name once, but he let go of Akeha's hand, let him leave with the troops. What choice did he have?

Chapter Twenty-two

THE SKY TURNED GRAY and heavy as they climbed the eight hundred steps to the Great High Palace, as though the heavenly host had amassed to bear witness. Akeha had spent the journey to the palace coming to a decision and making peace with it. He realized now that there was a reason he'd returned to the city today, and not any time before. His heart and veins were ice, and his mind was clear. He knew what he had to do.

The Protector met him in an open-air courtyard just off the main audience chamber. Akeha, trailing in the general's stiff-legged wake, was presented with a silent, heavily robed figure, hands folded behind her, gazing out at the white sprawl of the Great High Palace and the smoky tangle of Chengbee below.

"Protector, I have brought you the boy," the general said.

"Leave us," his mother said, without turning around.

"Yes, Protector." The general bowed and left.

The Protector continued studying the vista of her dominion, letting silence uncoil between them. Akeha was not intimidated. He scanned the courtyard for threats, his mindeye bright and open. Before him, his mother was a furnace in the Slack, a smear of light that was almost painful to focus on. They were truly alone.

She had let him come with weapons intact. All the knives tucked in easy corners. All the contents of his pockets. Hubris on her part, or foolishness? It did not matter.

"The sun falls and returns five times a day, the flowers wilt and return once a year. But the return of a wayward child is something that happens once a lifetime." The Protector turned around and took swaying, deliberate steps toward Akeha. "And here you are. Let me have a look at you."

The years had treated his mother well. Akeha, like everyone else, was not privy to her real age. She was supposed to have been in her fifties when the twins were born, which would put her in her eighties now. She didn't look it. She looked so much like Mokoya, big glassy eyes set in a broad, sharply contoured face.

It had been years since he'd stood in her presence. In that time, his life had been deformed around her and her actions. He had run from her troops. He had killed and watched others be killed. He had held the hands of dying friends, delivered bad news to grieving spouses and parents. He had seen families torn apart, watched the elderly starve, held children with all hope ripped from them.

And here she stood, radiant and triumphant, oblivious to the suffering that collected in the long shadow of her Protectorate. If his anger were poison, she would have been long dead.

The Protector clapped her hands to Akeha's face, her face crinkling in a smile of unverifiable sincerity. "See that. What a fine young man you have grown into."

He pulled his lips into a smile. "And I suppose you'll tell me how *proud* you are."

"Does it surprise you? There is greatness in your blood that cannot be denied."

Should he mock her for taking credit for his successes? No, that would just play into her game. "I'm not here for a warmhearted family reunion. Tell me what you want, or let me go."

The smile stayed on her face. "And of course, rude and ungrateful. As I have come to expect of you." She glided away, at ease in her seat of power. "All these years . . . did you think I knew nothing of what you have been doing? You and your sister both, with your charming little rebellion. All of which I indulged. I thought, why spoil the children's fun? But perhaps I have gone one step too far."

When she turned back, her smile had evaporated. "Very well. If you insist on acting like a grasping merchant, then let us lay out the terms of your surrender."

He indulged her: "What do you want?"

"Lady Han."

Akeha scoffed. "Do you imagine that I could go out, capture her, and bring her back tied in a red silk ribbon?"

"And give Mikara that sort of pleasure?" She blinked, like a crocodile. "Of course it won't be something so crude. You should know better that that, Akeha. Our arrangement will work this way. I will let you go. You may return to your sister and your little friends. Within you, implanted under your skin, will be a device developed by my Tensors that will send information back to us. It's simple enough. You don't even have to do anything."

Akeha pretended to think about it. Then he said, "No."

"No? Simply that?"

He nodded. "No."

"Ah." She laughed. "You haven't been in the capital for many years, Akeha. You think I'm giving you a *choice*."

He shrugged. "I'm *making* a choice."

"Your choice is between leaving the palace alive, and not."

"Accepting death is also a choice."

The Protector's face creased in mock concern. "Oh, but your sister's also dying, isn't she? Sonami tells me she needs a lung graft to survive. Who will be the donor if you die, I wonder?"

Sonami. The sudden mention of her name came like

a blow through the chest. Wasn't she supposed to be on their side?

He supposed it didn't matter.

"Would you truly sacrifice Mokoya as well?" she asked.

It was pathetic how little she knew of those she called her children. What they wanted. What they would choose.

Akeha turned away from her as though deep in thought. As though seriously considering her proposal. As he turned, he put his hand in his pocket, fingers brushing the cool petals of Eien's last gift to him. A gangrenous smile spread across his face. "You should have killed me when you could."

"Oh?" The Protector sounded amused. So much hubris. "And when should that have been?"

He laughed, a low sound. "You should have strangled me in the crib. The *spare child*, wasn't I? You should have gotten rid of me."

His fingers, burrowing deeper, closed around cold metal. A plum-sized metal sphere. "But you didn't. You let me grow up. You sowed the seeds of your own downfall. It's what you deserve."

He turned around, the sunball gleaming in his hand. His mother's eyes widened. "Is that . . ."

"Checkmate," he said.

He didn't have to do it *right*. Just enough to set it off. Akeha tensed.

In his hand the sunball flared to life. He hurled it forward, eyes closed, ready for his bones to dissolve in a blessing of heat and light.

The Slack *contracted*. The blow was so powerful he was flung off his feet. Was this what it was like to die?

And yet Akeha hit ground intact enough for it to hurt, muscle and tendon crying out at the impact of solid upon solid. The Slack flared nova-white, immense energy canceled out by immense energy.

His mother had countered the sunball.

Akeha leapt to his feet. The Protector lay crumpled a few yields away, an unmoving mound of silk and brocade. Was she dead? Had she sacrificed herself for him?

He moved toward her without thinking, bringing a knife to her throat. Not dead: his mother lay stunned, drained by her monumental expenditure of slackcraft. She looked up at him, pink-eyed, breathing shallowly, as his blade pressed into her skin.

He could just kill her. He should. Slit her throat and end this particular problem here and now. The flensing edge bit into her flesh. Blood welled up, bright against the metal.

She stared silently at him, a smile playing at her lips. Calm, almost proud.

Fury rampaged through him. He wanted her to say something. Anything. Insult him, plead with him, tell him she loved him. Explain why she'd protected both of them, instead of throwing the protective shield only around herself. *Anything.*

His hands shook. Red smeared over the edge of the metal.

He'd spent nearly twenty years running from her. He'd spent his entire life orbiting around her and his idea of her, distant as another galaxy. Even now, when he had her at the mercy of his blade, he wanted her to tell him what she was thinking, what she thought of him. She still had this power over him.

And then he knew. If he did the logical thing and pushed the knife all the way through her throat, if he stood by and watched while her blood emptied onto the gray flagstones and her pupils dilated into senselessness, if he gave in to his basest desires and slaughtered her right there—he could never leave. He would be trapped there forever, standing over his mother's dead body, his life from now on defined by this moment.

She would always own him. He would never be free.

There was always a choice.

Akeha straightened up. Her curious eyes followed him.

"I held your life in my hands," he said, his voice loud

and cold as ringing metal. "I could have killed you. Your fate belonged to me." He dropped the knife; it sang against the ground. "I choose to spare you. I release my hold over you."

He stepped backward, putting space between them. The Protector sat up slowly, a thin line of blood marking her neck. His mother said nothing. What did the look on her face mean? Was she confused, angry, happy? Did she think he was a fool or a hero? He couldn't tell. He couldn't read her expression. Perhaps he never could.

He said, "Now I turn my back, and I walk away. Whatever you do next is your choice. It will be your choice alone."

Akeha turned his back on his mother and began to walk.

He walked across the courtyard. Across its border and down the corridors where he had grown up. Any moment, he expected the claws of death to strike: a knife in the back, an arrow through the chest, the unbreakable grip of palace guards. Anything. Here were the ponds where he and Mokoya had spent afternoons chasing fish. There was the obelisk before which he first understood himself. With every minute, a different diorama from his past slid by, a reprise of all the opening gambits before the final moves were played. Any moment now.

Yet death still did not come. He was crossing the outer

pavilions, one step after another, heading forward. There was the threshold of the Great High Palace; there were the endless stairs that would lead him away from all this. He did not slow down. He did not look back. He put one foot in front of the other, a lone figure traversing the wide spaces that had once defined him. It had begun to rain, the gray skies finally shedding their load. The drops pelted him, warm and thick on his face. He tasted air full of earth and sky. Below him Chengbee waited, growing and breathing and alive.

Akeha walked and walked and walked.

EPILOGUE

IT WAS ONE WEEK, ten long days, before Mokoya allowed Akeha to see her. Thennjay found him meditating in the courtyard and said, "If you want to talk, I think she might say something now." She hadn't asked for him specifically, but there had been a softening in the baffling wall of thorns she'd woven around herself after she woke.

The first thing he heard was a rhythmic smacking sound, like a butcher tenderizing meat in a market square. Mokoya stood in the exercise yard, her back to him, repeatedly punching something that hung from a tree.

He approached her slowly. Her tunic had the sleeves cut off, exposing the fact that her right arm was now red and blue. Not the colors of beaten flesh, but of plumage and blossom, rich and deep. As Akeha drew closer, the lizard grain of the skin became apparent, supple and hairless, ridges of keratin rising and swirling down the rippling flesh.

Mokoya punched the flour bag with the lizard arm—five times, six—then shook it out like a child with pins and needles.

"Moko," he said.

She turned around. Saw him. Surprise, shock, then a carousel of unidentifiable emotions. A mass of scars crawled up the right side of her face, ropy and discolored.

She turned back to the flour bag without saying a word and started punching it again.

Akeha stood, waiting, while she struck out her anger, her grief, her frustration. Whatever demons clutched her in their grip. This was the Mokoya he remembered, full of emotion and impulse, always on her feet, always trying to think of something. On the streets of Jixiang and Cinta Putri and Bunshim, with the gulf of lakes and rivers between them, it had been so easy to turn her into this mythical figure, a distant and all-powerful entity insulated by the walls of the capital and the monastery. A prophet. *The* prophet. Beloved and abstract.

But she was also his sister. A mortal, a human being, a person. Made of flesh and sinew and bone and blood. And she could be hurt like anyone else.

Finally she let her arm hang loose, breathing hard. She didn't turn around. "I'm sorry I wasted your time."

"What do you mean? You didn't."

She cracked her knuckles. "You came because I was dying. You wanted to say good-bye, didn't you?" She started hitting the flour bag again, punctuating each word with a painful slapping sound. "But I didn't die." Smack.

Smack. "So you made the trip here for nothing."

He swallowed. "Not for nothing." She was a frenzied blur he was afraid to touch.

"Why else would you have come here? You could have done it, at any point. In the last eighteen years, Keha. At *any* point." She was crying now, her breaths wheezing through her chest, through her new lungs, grown from Akeha's own flesh. Her arm had changed color, stark yellow and black like a warning. She punched the bag twice more, so hard it swung like a pendulum, and rounded on Akeha. "You could have visited when she was alive. You could have met her."

"I know. Moko, I know. I'm sorry. I am so, so sorry."

She crumpled as the anger left her, and she allowed him to embrace her, allowed him to press her face into his chest as she wailed, pulling the fabric of his clothes into her balled fists. There was nothing he could say that would repair what had happened. Nothing could undo the fact that she had lost her daughter, her only daughter, the bright-eyed smiling girl that he had never met and now never would. He could only say, "I love you." He said the words, over and over and over. *I love you. I love you.*

Because Mokoya was still alive. Whatever the fortunes had woven, whatever the Almighty had willed, Mokoya had survived. Whatever Akeha could or couldn't do, he could love her. And love—that was all that had sustained them since they were children. Love, and nothing else. It was enough. As long as there was love, there would be hope. It was enough.

About the Author

Photograph by Nicholas Lee

JY YANG is a lapsed journalist, a former practicing scientist, and a master of hermitry. A queer, nonbinary, postcolonial intersectional feminist, they have over two dozen pieces of short fiction published in places including *Uncanny Magazine, Lightspeed, Strange Horizons,* and *Tor.com*. They live in Singapore, edit fiction at Epigram Books, and have a master's degree in creative writing from the University of East Anglia. Find out more about them and their work at jyyang.com, and follow them on Twitter: @halleluyang.

TOR · COM

Science fiction. Fantasy. The universe.

And related subjects.

*

More than just a publisher's website, *Tor.com* is a venue for **original fiction, comics,** and **discussion** of the entire field of SF and fantasy, in all media and from all sources. Visit our site today—and join the conversation yourself.